MAJOR LOT SMITH

MORMON RAIDER

IVAN J. BARRETT

To my wife, Minnie, whose uncle was a grandson of Lot Smith

Table of Contents

BOOK
1

BATTALION
BOY

CHAPTER 1

THE RAM IN THE THICKET—
PATRIOTISM

"**U**nited States soldiers!" exclaimed sixteen-year-old Lot Smith. Five men in uniform were riding into the Mormon encampment at Council Bluffs in July 1846. "What in tarnation are they here for?"

"Maybe Governor Ford told the truth for once," drawled Marshall Hunt, a youth of seventeen years. "He warned us Mormons if we ever tried going west, the President of the United States would send troops and hedge us up."

"If five men is all he's sending, we'll soon use 'em up," rejoined Lot. "But look, they're riding up to President Young's camp."

"So they are. Let's run over and find out why they're here." The two young Mormons ran toward Brigham Young's wagons, which were arranged in a circle near the hills of the high prairie crowding in upon the river. They were not alone in their curiosity.

Mothers left their washing of white muslins, red flannels, and multicolored calicos. Hurriedly they rinsed the articles of clothing they had in hand and hung them to dry upon the grass and bushes on the high banks of the stream. Then they hurried to the president's camp.

Herd boys, dozing upon the slopes on the north edge of the rich alluvial flat south of the encampment, left their sheep, oxen, cows, and horses and ran, shouting questions. Something more exciting than herding livestock was in sight. Four soldiers stood before the apostle's wagons. Within the log cabin which had been erected for a council house, the captain was consulting with Brother Brigham (as the pioneers affectionately called their leader) and other members of the Twelve Apostles.

Lot and Marshall, along with the herd boys and the others, gathered about the cabin and were anxiously waiting to discover the soldiers' purpose in meeting with the leaders. Could it be as Governor Ford had said, or was it a warning of Indian trouble? The latter seemed unlikely, as the Pottawatomie Indians seemed friendly and pleased to have the Mormons live among them.

A hush came over the crowd as President Young appeared in the doorway of the log council house with the army officer by his side. In a clear voice, he requested the anxious throng to meet in the bowery on the morrow at ten o'clock. He had important matters to bring to their attention.

Under Brother Brigham's direction, the men and boys had erected a large bowery—a fabrication of poles interwoven with slender branches and reeds and covered with a protective roof made of boughs with long bunch grass and covered with dirt. In the front end of this arbor was a rough table, behind which were wicker chairs made by the craftsmen of the Mormon colony.

Before the ten o'clock hour, two thousand anxious Saints gathered in and around the bowery. An American flag of thirteen stars and thirteen stripes had been hoisted on a tree used as a flagstaff near the front opening of the bowery. The leaders entered: Brigham Young, Heber C. Kimball, and Willard Richards in front, followed by Captain James Allen and two members of his staff. Following a prayer, President Young introduced Captain Allen to the large assembly.

Young Lot, near the front of the assemblage, carefully scrutinized the army captain. He seemed to be a plain, unassuming man without the proud, overbearing arrogance of the proverbial high-ranking military officer. Lot liked the man even before he addressed the gathering. A breathless silence came over the audience, and then Captain Allen spoke.

"My good people, I come to you in a spirit of helpfulness and friendship. Our country, as some of you may know, is at war with Mexico. Your help is needed. It is the request of the President of the United States that a battalion of five hundred men be raised from your number to go down and aid in the fight. I have been instructed by Colonel S. F. Kearney of the U.S. Army, now commanding the army in the West, to accept the service for twelve months of four or five companies of Mormon men who may be willing to serve their country for that period of time in our present war with Mexico. This force will unite with the army of the West at Santa Fe and be marched thence to California where they will be discharged.

"They will receive pay rations and other allowances, such as other regular soldiers receive, and will be entitled to all comforts and benefits of regular soldiers; and when discharged, they will be given gratis their arms and accoutrements with which they will be fully equipped at Fort Leavenworth. This is an opportunity for sending a portion of your young and intelligent men west for the benefit of your whole people and entirely at the expense of the United States. Those of you who are desirous of serving your country meet me shortly after this meeting. I will receive all healthy, able-bodied men from eighteen to forty-five years of age."

A low murmur of complaint and dismay was heard throughout the audience. What! A nation whose people had driven them from its borders, robbed them of their homes, and driven them into the wilderness to perish now called upon them for aid? Had not their oft-reiterated appeals for help to the president and Congress been denied?

Abraham Day, originally from Vermont, who was in his mid-twenties and had been in several scrapes with the Missouri Militia, voiced audibly the feelings of almost every man in the audience. "There is one man who will not go—d—n'em!"

And a young mother said loudly enough to be heard, "A more cruel demand could not be made upon us at this time of our affliction and poverty."

There were many apprehensions concerning the enlistment of five hundred volunteers. Brigham Young, Heber C. Kimball, and the other apostles felt at first that the call for their young men to march as soldiers to California was a gross injustice and an imposition upon the outcast Mormons. But as they thought it through, they began to see it differently.

As Captain Allen sat in the wicker chair behind the table, Brother Brigham arose. Unconsciously throughout the crowd, a feeling of confidence and peace replaced dismay.

"Attention all! The business to be laid before us is the call upon us from the War Department to furnish five hundred volunteers for the Army of the West to march to California. I am well acquainted with the situation of every man in the camp. At this time, surrounding circumstances must recede from our minds. Let them go. We may as well consider ourselves in good circumstances as bad ones! My experience has taught me it is best to do the things that are necessary and not keep my mind exercised in relation to the future. I have learned to do necessary things independent of my feelings and at the expense of everything near and dear to me. The blessings we are looking forward to will be attained through sacrifice.

"We want to raise the volunteers. Are we willing to undergo hardships and privation to procure that which we desire? I say we can do it.

"If we want the privilege of going where we can worship God according to the dictates of our conscience, we must raise the battalion. I say it is right, and who cares for sacrificing our comfort for a few years?

"This is the first time the government has stretched forth its hand to our assistance, and we receive their proffers with joy and thanksgiving. We feel confident our volunteers will have little or no fighting. The pay of the five hundred men will take their families west to them.

"The President of the United States has now stretched out his hand to help us, and I thank God and him too. It is for us to go, and I know you will go. I think the President has done us a great favor by calling upon us. It is the first call that has been made upon us that ever seemed likely to benefit us."

The feelings of the Saints became subdued as the words of Brother Brigham began to make sense to them. Men who had been resentful and angered at the request made by the army captain now saw the benefits amidst the required sacrifice.

To the women, it wasn't that easy. One young bride was heard to say, as her husband started to walk to the army officer who was in charge of the enlistment, "I don't want to be a soldier's widow."

But another young bride expressed the newly aroused spirit of the camp when she exclaimed courageously, "I'd rather be a soldier's widow than a coward's wife!"

The boys in their late teens were excited over the opportunity now offered them to become soldiers in the United States Army. Lot Smith was one of them.

The sensations of adventure tingled Lot Smith's spine; the feeling of service to country, God, and his people surged through his entire being. Like the rest of the Church members, he was destitute; the pay he'd get would take his parents to the Great Basin and, no doubt, help others journey westward. To his friends, Marshall Hunt and William Hendricks, he exclaimed, "I'm going to volunteer!"

"So am I," chimed in Marshall and William.

James S. Brown, a non-Mormon youth going west with the pioneers and not yet eighteen years of age, walked up. "While President Young was speaking, all those old stories of the Revolution, the War of 1812, and the Black Hawk Indian Wars flooded my mind. The spirit of the patriots awoke within me," he excitedly said, "and fellows, I'm going to serve my country!"

Although they respected Brother Brigham's judgment, sacrificing teamsters and manpower when the need was the most crucial didn't seem logical to some of the young men. "Brother Brigham declared he'd sooner have raised two thousand men a few weeks ago in twenty-four hours than one hundred now in two weeks," said James Bailey. He was a recent convert and friend of James Brown and Richmond Louder who were seriously considering following Bailey's steps and getting baptized. Would such a demand upon their young manhood hinder their intentions? "So many of our young men are in Missouri and parts of Iowa," continued Bailey, "working for the farmers to obtain food for their families."

"That's all right," chimed in Brown, "Richmond and I are here, and we'll go."

Bailey smiled, "You're a good one, and I'll join you. We'll be the best soldiers the U.S.A. ever had."

Elder Parley P. Pratt, who later accompanied the Battalion to Fort Leavenworth, overheard the men and walked up to them. He explained, "Brethren, the raising of the battalion is the 'ram in the thicket' for the Church. You recall the biblical story of Abraham and Isaac?"

"Yes, we know the story well."

"Isaac symbolized the Church—all set for the sacrifice. The knife is at his throat. A voice from heaven is heard! Poor Isaac is saved. Caught in the thicket is the ram. The ram is the battalion."

"The ram was the substitute for Isaac, but how is the battalion the ram for the Church?" asked Richard Bush.

Elder Pratt explained: "The Church is face to face with destruction. Financially we're ruined. President Young wanted to push an expedition west. It is too late now to do it even if five hundred recruits never marched. The Saints must winter here. Where's money to be had for the purchase of beef, blankets, flour? We must still move west, and we are forced to buy from our enemies in Missouri and Iowa—cash is the sole consideration with them. Did you notice Brother Brigham's face?"

"I'll never forget it. Few men ever faced a greater responsibility," James Bailey said.

"I readily see how the battalion can be the ram in the thicket," said William Hyde. William, a New Yorker by birth, and his father Herman heard the gospel, believed it and were baptized together on April 17, 1834. They went through all the trials in Missouri and fulfilled several missions in the eastern states before the expulsion of the Saints from Illinois. Now at age eighteen William would prove his patriotism when he joined that immortal body of men, the Mormon Battalion.

"Soldiers are paid in cash," chimed in Matthew Caldwell.

"Correct, but that's not all," voiced eighteen-year-old William. "Our patriotism should forever silence the accusations of the Mormons being enemies of the state. I hear numberwise we are furnishing ten times as many men proportionately to any state in the nation."

CHAPTER 2

LOT'S ENLISTMENT

Lot, having overheard Brother Pratt's explanation, mused, "'Ram in the thicket.' May I, young as I am, possess the virtues of a sacrificial ram!" He ran to his father's encampment. His father, William O. Smith, and his mother, Rhoda Hough Smith, were conversing with Jefferson Hunt, a forty-three-year-old man who had served as a major in the Nauvoo Legion and had also proven himself courageous in the Battle of Crooked River in Missouri. He was a tall, thin frontiersman with a stern countenance, but his blue eyes twinkled with good humor. His encampment was near the Smith's quarters. Jefferson Hunt had been in meeting with Brigham Young and members of the Twelve, and they had nominated him senior captain of the First Company of the battalion when the men were enlisted.

Lot could not restrain the feelings of his desire to join the battalion. His mother spoke up, "Lot, you are too young. Brother Hunt just told us the age for battalion recruits is eighteen to forty-five years."

"That won't keep me out. I overheard Brother Brigham say if we can't get enough young men over eighteen, we'll take the old men. If he'll take the old men, he'll also take the robust boys under eighteen, and I'm one of them. Marshall's going, isn't he, Captain Hunt?"

"Yes, I'll be taking my family with me."

After Captain Hunt departed, Lot's mother pled with him to give up his notion to enlist in the battalion. Lot's insistence caused his mother much concern. But knowing of his determination, she took the matter to the Lord in prayer. As she supplicated the Lord, a voice spoke to her saying, "Would you deprive your son of one of the greatest blessings he could have?"

She humbly said, "No, Lord."

The voice continued, "Then let your son go."

Lot's mother rose from her knees and sought out her son. "My son Lot, the Lord has made it known to me that you should go with the battalion, and I, your mother, give you my blessing. Go, my son, and God protect you."

The raven-haired youth took his mother in his arms and said, "Thank you, Mother. I will be a soldier you'll be proud of. My wages will take you and Father to the mountains. There we'll meet again and, as Brother Brigham said, 'worship God according to our conscience.'"

His mother answered, "I will pray for you daily, son, and if it is the Lord's will, we'll meet again in the Salt Lake Valley. Be a good soldier and remember your prayers."

Lot hurried to the bowery where the enlistment was taking place. Seeing the Stars and Stripes waving on the flagpole, he saluted and mused to himself, "I'll serve my country well!"

Isaac Carter stepped out of the bowery. Observing Lot he said, "The enlistment is over for today. You'll have to come back tomorrow if you want to enlist."

"Is that so?" snapped Lot. "How did you get enlisted so soon?"

"I was standing on that stump, and the recruiting officer walked over and asked, 'Do you want to go?' 'Yes,' I said, and he mustered me into service.""Well, I can do the same," exclaimed Lot, and he strode into the bowery. There behind the table sat Captain Allen and his aides. "Sir," said Lot, "I'd like to enlist in the army."

"We're pleased to have you, young man. Step over here, and we'll see if you're physically qualified."

During the physical examination, Lot stood on his tiptoes when he stepped under the line to measure his height. The examining officer smiled. "You needn't do that, lad. You're tall enough. We'll take you. By the way, what is your age?"

Lot gulped but quickly replied, "Sixteen years, sir, but I'm stronger than most eighteen-year-olds."

Captain Allen spoke up, "You are in fit condition, my boy, and we'll enlist you as the youngest soldier in the battalion. Be ready for duty tomorrow. You will be in Company E under Captain Daniel C. Davis."

"Yes, sir!" returned Lot.

CHAPTER 3

LIGHT-FOOTED LYDIA

At a farewell ball in the bowery, the pioneers temporarily forgot their sorrow for the moment and gave the battalion boys a send-off Lot never would forget. They danced to the musical tones of the violins, the cheerful sound of horns, the jingle of bells, and the "jovial snoring of the tambourine." Brigham Young and the other apostles with their wives threw off the heavy burdens pressing upon them and led off in the rhythmic steps and glides of a great double cotillion. Their lead in the dancing was the signal for others to join in the festivities. Light hearts, lithe figures, and nimble feet were joined by the venerated and merry grandparents who followed the fiddle to the fox-trot, French fours, Copenhagen jigs, and Virginia reels. The pioneers danced and made merry as they had done on festive occasions in Nauvoo; only now they were attired as mountain men and pioneer women. Even so, they wore their best homespun clothes, unless they had bartered them for food during the long march across Iowa.

Before their flight from Nauvoo these faithful women had sold their watches and trinkets as the most available resource for raising ready money. Although their ears were pierced and bore the loop marks of rejected pendants, the women were without earrings, finger rings, chains or brooches. Even without such ornaments, the women appeared appropriately dressed for such a celebration. The neatly darned white stockings and clean bright petticoats, the clear starched collars and chemisettes—perhaps faded only because they were too well washed by their pretty wearers—were evidence of better days, but not of more beautiful owners. On this ground, which had been trodden firm and hard, was gathered now the mirth and beauty of Mormon Israel.

Sixteen-year-old Lot watched the merriment and wished he were older. His father and mother were gaily stepping about with the apostles and their wives.

Across the bowery, Lot observed a group of teenage girls, sometimes pointing and giggling, as they watched the dancers. One of the girls, a graceful, pretty blonde, particularly caught his eye. The music stopped, and the dancers exchanged partners for the Copenhagen jig. Suddenly, the fair girl he had seen a moment before across the bowery stood directly before him. Without introduction she spoke to him, "Lot Smith, dance with me." Before Lot was conscious of what was happening, he was on the hard dirt floor dancing with the lovely girl who informed him that she was Lydia Burdick. During their dance, Lydia said seriously to Lot, "I am proud of you—so young and yet volunteering to march with the Mormon Battalion all the hard wilderness way to California."

Lot glanced at the pretty face so near him and replied, "It's not so much. What I'm doing is considered by Elder Parley Pratt as a ram in the thicket which will save the Church. You know, Lydia, the Church is destitute, and we battalion soldiers will help get you and all the rest of the pioneers to the Rocky Mountains. Brother Brigham told us we'd be discharged within eight hundred miles from the place he's taking you."

As Lot looked at his lovely dance partner, he noticed that her bare ears were pierced for earrings. Obviously, her girlish finery had gone to supply her family's needs. However, her neatly darned white stockings, bright petticoat, clean starched collar, and gingham gown fit her becomingly. Lot thought, "What a pretty girl you are." But aloud he remarked, "Lydia, you have lost your earrings."

"Oh, no—I sold them to an Iowa farmer to give to his wife in exchange for some corn and bacon to feed our family."

Lot feelingly said, "You are as fine a soldier in sacrificing as you say I am."

The music stopped; the Copenhagen jig had ended. Lot walked Lydia to the side of the bowery where her friends were standing and whispered in her ear before he left her, "Will you see us soldiers leave in the morning?"

Lydia smiled, and her blue eyes twinkled disarmingly, "I'll see you, Lot."

Now the party seemed all the merrier to Lot. He saw none who were not eager in following the fiddle to the Fox-chase Inn or Gardens of Gray's Ferry, figures performed with the spirit of people too happy to be slow, bashful, or unrestrained. Light hearts, agile bodies, and dexterous feet merrily swung about from an early hour till after the sun had dropped behind the sharp skyline of the Omaha hills.

Then silence was called for, and Susan Devine, a lovely young woman with a beautiful voice, sang a version of the psalm: "By the rivers of Babylon we sat down and wept. We wept when we remembered Zion." Accompanied by a string quartet, the notes came clear and vibrant. The words touched the hearts of the homeless Mormons. Many in the gathering expressed deep feelings, and tears moistened almost every eye. The song ceased. Breaking the quiet, the deep voice of an elder invoked the blessings of heaven upon those who would depart with the battalion and the many who were to remain.

The Pottawatomie Indians had also taken part in the festivities. They had welcomed the pioneers and allowed them to live on their land. Decked in scarlet blankets and feathered leggings, these Indians loitered to the last, seemingly unwilling to adjourn to their own village.

Most of the Saints had dispersed, but Lot and his friend Willard Smith lingered. Willard had played with the dance band and seemed loathe to leave as did Lot. Tomorrow both of these lads would start their march with the Mormon Battalion. Lot saw Brother Brigham near the front entrance to the bowery with Apostles Taylor and Woodruff. They were accompanied by a handsome stranger, a slightly built young man in his mid-twenties. His black, wavy hair was joined with sideburns and an oval beard. On his upper lip he sported a well-groomed mustache. They were conversing with Lot's father and mother who had been waiting for their son. Lot and Willard walked to where the Church leaders and the stranger were talking with William and Rhoda Smith. Brigham Young observed the two boys, greeted them, and addressing the young stranger, said, "Colonel Kane, here are two of our Mormon boys who have enlisted in the battalion. This boy," he said as he pointed to Lot, "is only sixteen years of age, but he is a steady, level-headed youth." Brigham Young then looked at Willard. "Willard is nineteen and is the son of widow Amanda Smith, whose husband and ten-year-old son were murdered by a Missouri mob. Boys, meet Colonel Thomas L. Kane, who came all the way from Washington alone with important dispatches from the President of the United States. He would like to go to the Rocky Mountains with us."

"Young men, I am pleased to make your acquaintance, "said Colonel Kane. Kane was a handsome young attorney who was a close associate of President James K. Polk. "I know your leaders are proud of you. What I have seen this afternoon is an example of your noble self-denial and your willingness to suffer for conscience's sake. You Mormons will leave upon my mind an abiding impression that there is something higher and better than pursuing earthly treasures. God bless you on your march to California," concluded Colonel Kane.

Lot spoke for himself and Willard with his reply, "Thank you, Colonel Kane. We shall not forget you, and I feel that we'll meet you again after the war."

President Young said, "Lot, we have much confidence in you; and I feel in the future, when we all get into the Rocky Mountains, you'll do an important service for the Church and its people. By the way, while Colonel Kane is with us, he will stay with your parents and will occupy the bed you'll vacate when you depart with the battalion."

With considerable animation Colonel Kane, addressing all present, exclaimed, "What a farewell ball you had! The orchestra astonished me by its numbers and fine drill. I understand one of your eloquent Mormon missionaries converted those musicians in a body at an English town, and they followed him with their trumpets, trombones, and drums to America."

President Brigham Young pointed to Wilford Woodruff and said, "Colonel Kane, here is that eloquent missionary—one of our Twelve Apostles."

Wilford commented, "They are not only accomplished musicians but humble Saints as well. A number of them, along with Willard here, will be marching with the battalion and will inspire the soldiers with their martial music on the march to California."

"Young brethren," broke in President Brigham Young, "this march to California will be strenuous and trying. You will face hardships aplenty. Remember to keep faithful and live your religion, and the Lord will bless you with strength and courage to endure. You are ready for greater blessings and greater responsibilities. I feel to ordain you elders in the Melchizedek Priesthood, which is after the order of the Son of God."

The two young men suddenly felt nervously unworthy but grateful that Brother Brigham felt they were ready to receive this high advancement in the holy priesthood. Lot was invited to sit first in one of the wicker chairs. He felt the hands of Brother Brigham and the other apostles upon his head and heard the voice of the chief apostle confer the higher priesthood upon him and then ordain him to the office of elder in that priesthood. Many gifts and blessings were pronounced upon him with the promise that he should have power to heal the sick and denounce evil. The pronouncement of "amen" concluded the simple but solemn rite. In a like manner, Willard Smith's ordination followed. Colonel Thomas L. Kane looked on with respect and wonderment.

Brother Brigham placed his hands on the shoulders of the two young men and said, "Good night. God bless you and keep you."

CHAPTER 4

THE GOODBYE

Early the following morning, the young men and boys who had enlisted in the United States Army were in line according to companies. Youthful patriotism abounded as they readied themselves to start a two hundred mile march to Fort Leavenworth, their first destination. Lot was surprised to see attached to the battalion some twenty-five wives of officers and their children, along with some older men and women. For such to set out on a march to California over rugged, unknown country was a stupendous undertaking, and Lot sensed the seriousness of it as never before.

"Attention, battalion soldiers." It was the voice of Captain Allen. "You soldiers will receive a clothing allowance instead of being issued uniforms. You will be paid three dollars and fifty cents a month. Each soldier will carry his own clothing, blanket, greatcoat, shirt, pantaloons, and socks and shoes. Blankets can be procured from Mr. Sarpy, the Indian trader. He will sell them for a price as low as you can get them in St. Louis, and he'll wait for his payment until it can be deducted from the men's pay. You will also want knives."

President Brigham Young then addressed the Mormon soldiers. Lot observed the leader carefully. He was a man in the prime of a hale and vigorous manhood, although the responsibilities of leading the Saints out of Nauvoo had taken a toll—his face had a haggard appearance and he had lost too much weight. Standing before his brethren who had so willingly accepted the call to serve their country, his five-foot-ten-inch frame seemed stooped, but his exuberant vitality and unswerving faith in the cause and in himself were still evident. His regular, well-formed features were sharp, and he was smiling. His words came easily without affectation. He instructed the young men to manage their affairs by the power and influence of the priesthood, "and you'll have power to preserve your lives and the lives of your companions and escape difficulties." He then pledged with his right hand raised to the square that every man would return alive if he performed his duties faithfully, without murmuring. "Go in the name of the Lord and be humble and pray every morning and evening in your tents."

Sixteen-year-old Lot felt as important as Captain Jefferson Hunt when Brother Brigham said, "A private soldier is as honorable as an officer. No one is distinguished as being better flesh and blood than another. Honor the calling of every man in his place. Keep neat and clean, teach chastity, gentility, and civility; swearing must not be allowed, insult no man; have no contentious conversations with the Missourians, Mexicans, or any other class of people. Do not preach, only when people desire to hear, then be wise; impose not your principles upon any people; take your Bibles and Books of Mormon; burn your playing cards if you have any. When your Heavenly Father has proved that a man will be his friend under all circumstances, he will give to that man abundantly and withhold no good thing from him." He assured the Mormon soldiers they'd have no fighting except with wild animals. President Young and all the apostles bade them an affectionate farewell with "God bless you and spare your lives."

Lot looked over the large gathering of Saints who were there to bid the soldiers farewell. He saw his father and mother, and there, standing nearby, was Lydia, who, observing him looking her way, waved her hand. He waved back. Following a prayer, the ten musicians in the battalion, directed by Levi W. Hancock who was one of the seven presidents of the Seventy and the only General Authority marching to California, struck up the popular but poignant tune, "The Girl I Left Behind Me." The Mormon Battalion boys stepped out of Council Bluffs in time and commenced their march toward the Missouri River and Sarpy's Post where they would get their blankets. Crowds of mothers, wives, sweethearts, and fathers waved and sobbed their goodbyes. William Casper, one of Lot's comrades, saw his young wife with their baby in her arms near the line of march. He said to her as he slackened his step, "Sarah Ann, you are in the hands of the same God as I am. May he bring us together again."

Those words sank deeply into young Lot's soul. "We all are in the hands of God. He will see us through," he said to himself. Lot thought of Lydia. She was pretty and graceful, her face radiant, her personality becoming, her faith firm in the Mormon cause. The touch of her hand had pricked him with thrilling sensations; her very presence enthralled him. "I shall not forget her," he mused. "Lydia Burdick, I shall one day claim you as my wife." Keeping step with the other troopers, he continued to hum the tune after the battalion band ceased to play, and the words of the last verse filled his entire being:

> My mind her form shall still retain,
> In sleeping or in waking,
> Until I see my love again
> For whom my heart is breaking.
> If ever I shall see the day,
> When Mars shall have resigned me,
> Forever more I'll gladly stay,
> With the girl I've left behind me.

CHAPTER 5

THE MARCH BEGINS

During the latter part of July 1846, the battalion passed through towns and villages in Missouri along the river south to Fort Leavenworth. The heat was oppressive and the roads dusty. With only a small ration of food, Lot and his fellow soldiers suffered much from empty stomachs. Their strength and endurance were lessened. However, an unsurpassed spirit of brotherly love and union abounded. Placing their all on the altar of sacrifice for God, his kingdom, and their country, the youthful soldiers marched daily in heat and summer rainstorms, and not a dissenting voice was heard. Lot and others peeled bark off trees to form a kneading trough in which to make their scant flour into bread dough, after which the dough was rolled into sticks and held over the campfire. The half rations given the soldiers were badly or insufficiently cooked for lack of proper utensils. Lying on the ground at night with only one blanket each, one young battalion member said, "It is a wonder the entire camp is not down sick. Everything seems to move harmoniously among the men."

On the morning of the third day of marching from Sarpy's Point, Lot and his fellow battalion members had the painful duty of burying Samuel Boley of Company B. He had died of cholera. Lot knew him to be not much older than himself, a young man of integrity and energy. Lot helped wrap him in his blanket and assisted in his burial in a rough lumber coffin, the best the battalion could obtain. During Samuel's illness, he had been kindly attended to by the assistant surgeon, Dr. William L. McIntyre. Two days following the death of Private Boley, many of the battalion soldiers retired to their blankets on the ground fasting since they were without flour. Crossing the Nodawey River, the battalion camped at Oregon, Missouri. Here a Missourian drove up with a load of flour but refused to deliver the flour to the quartermaster because he was a Mormon. "I will deliver it only to the Colonel," he decidedly announced. Colonel Allen was highly disgusted when informed of the ornery Missourian and ordered the flour be delivered immediately to the quartermaster. "If the Missourian doesn't comply, I'll arrest him and put him under the Mormon guard."

Lot shouted, "Good for the Colonel!" and all the battalion echoed "God bless the Colonel."

Passing through Missouri villages, the Mormon soldiers saw many of the old mobocrats who expressed regret that they had persecuted the Mormons. They welcomed them back into Missouri and were dumbfounded to observe the Mormon Battalion with their perfect order and civility.

Lot carried a makeshift calendar in his pocket and noted on 29 July that he and the battalion marched through St. Joseph to the tune of "The Girl I Left Behind Me." On the last day of July, the soldiers along with the families of the officers reached the thriving Missouri town of Weston, which was across the river from Fort Leavenworth. It took five hours for the battalion to ferry across the muddy stream and make its way to the garrison.

Lot observed that beyond the Missouri River, with its thick borders of cottonwood and box elder trees, there were no trees growing around Fort Leavenworth. The tall bluestem grass grew almost waist high, and the shorter buffalo grass covered the ground. This heavy growth of herbage, suitable for grazing animals, was not diminished by the U.S. horses and mules at the fort. A soft breeze coming from the south cooled the hot faces of the battalion members. "This is Kansas," declared Levi Hancock in Company E, "named for the Kan or Kansa Indians who once roamed this prairie. The name means 'the people of the south wind.'"

"That's good to know," said Lot. "Look at these tall, yellow sunflowers growing with the bluestem grass."

Fort Leavenworth had been built nineteen years before the arrival of the battalion by Colonel Henry H. Leavenworth to protect the wagon trains passing over the Santa Fe Trail. The cantonment of log huts with a log fortification built by Leavenworth had been expanded by the United States Army. Within a fortified enclosure covering twenty acres were a score or more log and slab cabins to house the soldiers stationed there in the most important army post on the western frontier.

All was bustle and activity at Fort Leavenworth. This was the outfitting station for the United States troops at war with Mexico. Steamboats were unloading food, equipment, and necessary materials; teams drawing wagons loaded with these materials taken off the steamboats filled the streets. Squads of soldiers were being drilled; the sound of the bugle, the beating of the drums accompanied by the shrill notes of the fifes, and the tramp, tramp of the army men as they were trained for combat frequently reached the ears of Lot and his company. Many of the new recruits from Missouri, Illinois, and other states were rough and uncultivated in appearance and behavior. Drinking and fighting seemed to be their major pastimes. Lot and his companions were amazed and shocked at the profane and vulgar language and vile actions they were compelled to listen to and view.

The battalion camped on the public square inside the fort. Army personnel headed by Colonel Allen brought one hundred tents for the Mormons, one for every six privates. Lot was assigned to the tent with two other Smith boys who, like himself, had good Bible names, David and Elisha. David Pettigrew, the oldest man in the battalion was also assigned to Lot's tent. He was fifty-five years old. This assignment was possibly made to balance the age level, Lot being under the age limit and Pettigrew beyond it. David Pettigrew and forty-three-year-old Levi W. Hancock had been appointed by President Brigham Young to counsel, advise, and act as fathers to the battalion boys. Elder Hancock was the chaplain of the battalion. Although Levi was not considered a private since he was chief musician and chaplain, Lot was pleased to learn that he would be the sixth occupant of the tent.

Each company had four women as laundresses, who were soon busy washing soldiers' clothing in a stream near the fort. The soldiers also drew camp equipment and rations from the government. Lot drew a flintlock musket with bayonet, twenty-four cartridges, a belt, and cartouches. He was equipped with a haversack to carry over his shoulder, a knapsack, and provisions.

Lot and other young soldiers were anxious to receive their first guns. Observing this, Colonel Allen said in his good-natured, humorous way, "Stand back, boys; don't be in a hurry to get your muskets. You'll want to throw the darn things away before you get to California."

Lot received forty-two dollars for clothing. Most of the money he sent back to Council Bluffs with Elder Parley P. Pratt for the support of his family. Elder Pratt, who had accompanied the battalion for this very purpose returned to Council Bluffs with $5,860. The members of the battalion had not forgotten their families. The paymaster remarked that every member of the Mormon Battalion could write his own name, while only one-third of the volunteers he had previously paid could.

The battalion boys trusted Colonel Allen and respected every word he spoke. One day Lot overheard him say to an officer, "I have not been under the necessity of giving the word of command to the Mormons a second time. The men, though unacquainted with military tactics, are willing to obey orders."

Not long after the battalion arrived, Lot, Willard Smith, James S. Brown, Marshall Hunt, and other young men were returning from drill to the battalion encampment on the square when they came upon two half-drunk, Missouri ruffians who were fighting. One struck his opponent on the forearm with a sharp hatchet he had in his hand. Blood gushed forth, and the bewhiskered victim cried in pain. The fellow with the hatchet raised it high above his head intending to finish the wounded fellow. Lot, observing this, rushed up and grabbed the wrist of the drunken ruffian. Lot gave the man's wrist a violent twist and the hatchet fell to the ground. Willard snatched it up and held it firmly. The startled Missourian wheeled around sharply. Seeing Lot and six other Mormon soldiers, he swore with an oath and sneeringly threatened, "I'll get my Missouri comrades, and we'll use you d— Mormons up."

"No, you won't!" defied Lot. "Run for Doc Sanderson and have him take care of this Missourian you tried to kill."

Swearing, the ruffian staggered to the hospital cabin.

Willard looked at the hatchet he had in his hand and gasped, "This is my father's hatchet. There are his initials on the oak handle." He pointed to the letters "W.S."

The Mormon boys made a tourniquet with a shirt and a stick and put it on the wounded man's arm to stop the bleeding. Dr. George B. Sanderson, accompanied by the ruffian and five other Missourians, arrived with his medical kit. Sanderson had been assigned as surgeon for the battalion. He was a Missourian from Platte County and proved to be cruel and tyrannical. He regularly incurred the ill will of the Mormon soldiers on their long march to California.

As the Missourians lifted the wounded man and began to carry him to the hospital cabin, the dark-bearded, coarse-featured Missourian demanded the hatchet. Willard defiantly refused to give it to him. "This is not your hatchet," he said. "It belonged to my father whom you killed at Haun's Mill." The dark face of the man turned ashen white. He gasped as he stared at Willard. "You're not his . . .?"

"Yes, I am," replied Willard.

The Missourian turned abruptly and fled muttering, "O my god! O my god!"

A small band of Mexican mules was brought to the fort to be used as teams to transport necessities and carry the families of the battalion members. These mules were wild and unbroken and unaccustomed to the harness. Some of the young Mormon men from each company were assigned to harness these onery animals. Lot was one of the boys assigned from Company E to break the mules. To his surprise, he saw one of those little, long-eared beasts dragging five men around the fort enclosure. Lot, a strong youth, thought he could handle one of the little mules himself. His conceit was soon humbled as he was jerked and dragged by one of the wiry little mules, burning his hand severely with the rope.

"Lad, let me handle that little cuss," someone said, as the animal drug Lot across the yard. "I'll show you how to tame him down." A large man with huge hands stepped up and grabbed the long ears of the animal. He twisted them slightly and the bucking, kicking quadruped became calm and submitted to the harness. With the assistance of the stranger, the Mormon Battalion boys accomplished the task, but not before they were frustrated and tired. They thanked the stranger for his help. The big fellow smiled, showing two missing front teeth, and, extending his right hand, introduced himself. "I'm Jack Bennington from Indiana. I came out here to help in the war, but observing you fellows in the Mormon Battalion, I'd like to join up and march with your companies to California."

"You'll need to contact Captain Jefferson Hunt about joining up with us," said Lot. "He is over by his tent at the further end of the square."

Reaching Captain Hunt, Bennington made his request. Captain Hunt said, "One of our men died a few days ago, which left a vacancy in Company B. You can see Captain Jesse D. Hunter of that company, and he'll fix you up."

Jack Bennington was pleased. He said, "I'd like to join you Mormons and be baptized into your church."

Captain Hunt continued, "Lot will take you to Elder Levi W. Hancock, our chaplain, and he will instruct you and inform you regarding the requirements for church membership."

That evening, while Lot and his five tentmates gathered for prayers, Levi W. Hancock informed them that he had talked with Bennington and found him sincere. "Tomorrow, brethren, we'll baptize Jack Bennington in the Missouri River. I'd like you all to go with us for the baptismal service after our morning drill."

About noon the next day, the six soldiers walked to the Missouri River. Finding a secluded spot below the ferry crossing, Levi took the man into the water and performed the ceremony. On raising Bennington from the water, Levi was deeply stirred by the spirit and said, "If I have baptized a murderer, it will do him no good." His words had such an effect upon the stranger that later that day he confessed to Brother Hancock that years before he had killed his brother. He was a murderer.

On the long and tedious march, Levi's wise counsel and exemplary course did much to mold the character of the soldiers. Being in the same company and tent with him, Lot felt his influence and listened to his deliberations under every circumstance.

CHAPTER 6

ON THE TRAIL TO SANTA FE

Sunday was observed with worship services by the battalion soldiers and the families of the officers. Lieutenant George P. Dykes of Company D preached a military gospel sermon. The weather was hot; many of the men were sick from ague. During the service the soldiers prayed for the sick. They prayed a special prayer for their beloved Colonel James Allen, who was seriously ill. He was well liked and their wasn't a soul in the camp who didn't send a few words to heaven in his behalf. At the services, Lot saw Jack Bennington at the back of the gathering. After the services Lot tried to reach him, but Jack eluded him and any other LDS battalion member who knew him. Bennington dropped out of the battalion before Lot ever had a chance to speak with him again.

When Colonel Allen saw that he wasn't going to get better quickly, he instructed Captain Hunt to advance with the battalion toward Santa Fe while he remained at the fort and recuperated. He, with Lieutenants George P. Dykes and Samuel Gally who were charged to remain with him, would overtake them later. Lot, with James S. Brown and Willard Smith, stopped at the door of the hospital cabin to bid their revered colonel goodbye. The colonel raised himself from his bed and bade them enter. He returned their sharp salute.

"Boys," he said, "I have been much impressed with you, your courage, and your faith. I hope very soon to be with you again. Before you leave, offer a prayer for me." Lot looked at James and Willard. They nodded to him to do the praying. The three boys knelt at the Colonel's bed, and Lot implored the Lord in all his youthful faith and sincerity for the immediate recovery of their Colonel.

Tears trickled down Colonel Allen's cheeks. "Thank you, my soldiers! Goodbye, and God bless you."

The route of travel lay over rolling hills, through partly timbered country and prairie. The weather was uncomfortably warm and sultry. Many of the soldiers and some women and children suffered from ague. Chills and fever plagued them all during the long, slow journey to Santa Fe. Each company was supplied with one large wagon pulled by four yoke of oxen which carried the tents, camp equipage, and rations for one week. The battalion's commissary and ammunition division included over one hundred wagons, with four pieces of artillery pulled by mules in the rear. These were under the command of a wagon master and assistants.

On August 17, five days out from Fort Leavenworth, Delaware and Shawnee Indians ferried the battalion members and wagons across the Kaw River, which was four hundred yards wide. The Indians grew good crops of corn and watermelon. Lot and his young companions bartered with the Indian farmers for vegetables.

"Heap good Indian," said Lot, "You know Mormons?"

"Nope, me no know Mormon," answered one buck with a grunt.

"You remember many moons ago paleface Mormon Cowdery telling you about Indian book of forefathers?"

An elderly male Indian standing nearby smiled, "Me remember! Heap good paleface. Our Chief Anderson like Mormon book of our forefathers. The chief's father was a Scandinavian who married an Indian princess. His name was Anderson and the chief retained the name as his own."

Lot pulled a copy of the Book of Mormon from his haversack on his back and handed it to the big Indian. "Me give you for much corn, watermelon."

"Okay, you have much!"

Lot, with the other Smith boys, Elisha, David, and Luther, gathered a large quantity of corn on the cob and watermelon and hurriedly loaded them in the company E supply wagon. "Thank you, and God bless you," said Lot as he and the others ran to catch up with their company.

A few miles beyond the Kaw River the battalion endured the severest storm of rain and wind Lot had ever been through. The wind blew down the majority of the tents, overturned six government wagons, and rolled several others as if they were tumbleweeds.

"Fall on your faces," Lot yelled to his tent mates, "or you'll be blown away!"

The older men immediately obeyed. "Good advice, Lot," gray-haired David Pettigrew yelled.

Everyone was soaked to the skin and some were frightened, but none were hurt more than getting a good soaking.

The next day, a messenger arrived from Fort Leavenworth with the sorrowful news of the death of their commander, Colonel James Allen. It was a sad blow to the men of the battalion. They had loved him and their spirits grieved. Lot was especially upset. "I probably didn't have the faith required for his recovery," he sobbed.

"I don't feel that way, Lot," replied Private Christopher Layton, a British convert, of Company C. "Colonel Allen's demise was the act of a benevolent Providence, for his nature was too kind and sympathetic to have forced his men through what us Mormon Battalion boys will have to endure before we reach California."

Lot thought about what Christopher said. Captain Hunt called the companies together in a memorial assemblage to honor their deceased commander. Lieutenant George P. Dykes preached a lavish eulogy, choosing the resurrection for his text.

A few days later, the battalion received the news that Lieutenant Colonel Samuel D. Smith of the regular army would be their commander. The soldiers had not been consulted when the command was given to Lieutenant Colonel Smith by Major Horton of Fort Leavenworth. The men were not happy with the decision; they felt that it was Captain Jefferson Hunt's official right to exercise of authority over the Mormon Battalion.

Smith brought with him Dr. George D. Sanderson who was soon loathed by every Mormon soldier. And after experiencing Colonel Allen's leadership, the men found they could hold very little respect for Smith. At the time Smith took over command, there was much sickness in camp—chills, fever, and mumps. These illnesses were brought on by contaminated drinking water and poorly cooked food. Under Colonel Allen, sick men had been permitted to crawl into the company wagon, but pompous, ungentle LtC. Smith, with threats and oaths, pulled the sick men out of the wagons because they had neglected to report to Dr. Sanderson. In front of all the soldiers, the arrogant commander directed that before any sick soldier could ride he must be reported by the doctor as unable to walk. Every morning each sickly man or boy, whether he could walk or not, had to go see Dr. Sanderson, who sat in front of his tent with a medicine book on his knee. A long chest full of medicine rested on the wagon tongue near the doubletrees; a black man stood nearby acting as a bodyguard, and a hospital steward stood in front of the wagon. When a man's name was called, the hospital steward was ordered to give him a dose of calomel or arsenic or a decoction of bayberry bark and camomile flowers. Any one of these concoctions was enough to kill any ordinary man. Sanderson's potions were poured into the mouths of the sick soldiers with an old, uncleaned iron spoon which he considered "good enough for the Mormons." The soldiers' instructions from Brother Brigham had been: "If you are sick, live by faith, and leave the surgeon's medicine alone if you want to live, using only such herbs and mild food as are at your disposal. If you heed this counsel, you will prosper." But LtC. Smith and Dr. Sanderson compelled the sick Mormons to take their drugs. The sick soldiers unable to walk to the sick call received not only the medicine but the cursing of the red-faced, bewhiskered Sanderson. No other Americans would have submitted to the tyranny and abuse that the Mormon Battalion received from Smith and Sanderson. The battalion would not have stood for it except, as Lot said to a group of his fellow soldiers, "We are servants of our God and patriots to our country."

For seven weeks under Smith's command, the battalion soldiers plodded doggedly through the suffocating heat and dust of the Kansas prairie. The officers, wives, and their children came along behind in slow-moving wagons drawn by mules, They traveled through deserts and over mountains. There were days without water and days without sufficient food. Yet they marched on. Lot and his fellow soldiers were tired and footsore. They suffered intensely from heat and lack of water. The thirsty soldiers saw mirages which appeared as fog rising from water and then looked like a lake of clear water. Lot's company passed one pond full of insects out of which they drove a thousand buffalo. The soldiers put the water in vessels and sucked it out through a silk handkerchief. One of the soldiers killed a buffalo. The meat was pretty good eating. Their only fuel was buffalo chips, which were scarce, as many travelers had gone this way before.

One hundred miles from Fort Leavenworth the battalion reached the Arkansas River, which was about a quarter of a mile wide and filled with sand. Here and there trickled a small, brackish stream of water. After crossing the river bed, the battalion camped. The men dug holes three feet deep in the sand and got enough water for drinking and for the laundresses to wash the clothes. Lot and the younger soldiers speared a number of fish in the shallow water with their swords and bayonets. Both soldiers and families relished their suppers that evening.

While camped on the Arkansas, Lieutenant Smith ordered a number of the officer's families to be sent to Pueblo for the winter because they were slowing the progress of the battalion. Some of the officers opposed this move, but Lieutenant Dykes agreed with the commander. Captain Nelson Higgins of Company D along with a guard of ten men was assigned to take the families north up the Arkansas River to Pueblo.

On the evening of their departure, Private Alva Phelps of Company E died. Lot had marched by his side much of the distance from Fort Leavenworth. Just before reaching the Arkansas, Phelps became weary and wished to rest, but Sanderson insisted he take his strong medicine. Private Phelps begged the doctor not to give him any medicine. Alva insisted that all he needed was a little rest and then he'd be able to return to duty. With horrid oaths, Sanderson forced him to take his calomel and arsenic from the old, rusty spoon. A few hours later, he died. Lot and every member of the battalion felt that the quack, who posed as a doctor, had killed him. Alva was buried on the south bank of the Arkansas river. After dark a new star appeared in the eastern sky, dancing up and down directly in the course the battalion travelled. Finally the star sank out of sight. To Lot the star was a sign that the Lord had welcomed home his young soldier, Alva Phelps.

Nearly a third of the men were afflicted with malaria or diarrhea. The army had made no provision for hauling sick men. Wagons and mules of necessity had the task of handling provisions and military equipment. Whether the men were sick or well, Smith mercilessly drove them forward. Once, during a brief rest, Lot voiced the feelings of many: "It looks as if the Lieutenant and surgeon are determined to kill us with these forced marches." That evening the Mormon officers held a council with the battalion's spiritual advisers, Levi W. Hancock and David Pettigrew, to discuss what could be done to ameliorate the circumstances of the sick men. Chaplain Hancock and the oldest man in the battalion, David Pettigrew, appealed to Lieutenant Smith, but he heartlessly replied that he could do nothing.

Lot and a number of the battalion soldiers pooled their meager cash and purchased a wagon and a team of mules at a bargain price from wayfarers on the Santa Fe trail for the purpose of conveying the sick brethren. The next morning at sick call, Sanderson reported to Smith that four of the sickest soldiers were absent. Lieutenant Smith found them in the wagon which Lot and the others had purchased. He demanded, "What the hell right have you got hauling men in this wagon?"

Lot replied, "These men are sick. We bought this wagon to carry the sick, and I'm going to haul them. Lieutenant, you have disgraced the name of Smith by your disgraceful treatment of the men in this battalion, and I'll be d—d but what I'll uphold the Smith name by showing a little mercy. No more of my brethren are dying from Sanderson's poison or for lack of rest; they'll ride."

With an oath Lieutenant Smith jerked out his sword and threatened the sixteen-year-old private. Lot grabbed a tent peg and told his commander to come ahead. Smith departed in a rage and Lot expected to be court-martialed, but surprisingly, nothing more was said of the incident by the commander. Lot and his tentmates continued to haul the sick in their newly purchased wagon.

Lot's duty as a soldier was not solely to tramp all day with musket, accoutrements, and knapsack while the sickly soldiers rode and rested in the newly acquired wagon; he also had to push and pull wagons uphill, hold them back when going down hill, push them through drifting sands, and assist in getting the wagons and teams out of quicksand. Often during the night, he stood guard or helped herd the stock. Day after day he and his fellow soldiers pressed on.

Each evening when not on night duty, Lot enjoyed the companionship of his tentmates. His mother had given him half-dozen large tallow candles before he marched out of Council Bluffs. "Son, I'm giving you these candles so in the evenings you can read your Bible and Book of Mormon," she told him. By the flickering candlelight at the request of Lot and other soldiers, Elder Levi W. Hancock read the scriptures to them. After scripture reading, Father Pettigrew led in the evening devotional.

One evening, Levi read the description of the Lamanite soldiers under command of Helaman:

> And they were all young men, and they were exceedingly valiant for courage, and also for strength and activity; but behold, this was not all—they were men who were true at all times in whatsoever thing they were entrusted.
>
> Yea, they were men of truth and soberness, for they had been taught to keep the commandments of God and to walk uprightly before him. (Alma 53:20-21)

Following a pause after the reading, the youthful Lot commented, "We, in the Mormon Battalion, are much like Helaman's young soldiers. We have been taught to keep the commandments of God, and we are trying to walk uprightly before him, in spite of that insolent commander and obnoxious medical quack."

Elder Hancock agreed. "Let us keep our faith and courage," he said. Lot was even more resolved to be a good soldier and to be true to his church and country.

After an arduous march of twenty miles over rough roads and deep sand, and through the sinks of Cimmaron River (in what is now the state of New Mexico), the battalion camped at Gold Springs where there was good water and timber. Mountain peaks were around them— the first mountains many of the soldiers, including Lot, had ever seen. Here the hungry Mormon men added turkey, antelope, and bear to their scanty diet.

The battalion met an express of large Santa Fe wagons whose drivers informed them that General Kearney had taken the Mexican town of Santa Fe without firing a shot and that the battalion soldiers were to march directly to Santa Fe.

The mountain air was bracing to the battalion, though many of their number remained sick. Lieutenant Colonel Smith and the doctor assembled those considered able to stand for a forced march to Santa Fe. The sick were left behind to care for themselves and to look after the broken-down teams.

Lot had endured the march very well. He had not succumbed to the sicknesses which had afflicted many of the soldiers. His friend and fellow soldier James S. Brown was given a night guard; although badly afflicted with diarrhea, he stood guard in a heavy downpour of rain rather than crawl to Doc Sanderson for calomel and arsenic. However, the next day he was on the sick list. The "sick wagon" was left in his charge and Lot, with the others who had purchased it were ordered to make the hurried march to Santa Fe.

With feed and water plentiful, the jaded animals perked up each day. The marching soldiers felt an upsurge of energy and vitality even though every monotonous step was a trial to sixteen-year-old Lot. Left, right, left—hour after hour. Count one, two, three—until a thousand was reached, then he'd start to count again. What a tedium of figures! His feet, stabbed by rocks, pained him; his shoulders chafed from the heavy knapsack. Thirty miles of tramping on blistered feet came to an end at the village of Las Bayas. It was only a cluster of low, flat adobe huts, but the humble village interested Lot and gave him relief. The small Mexican sheep and goats amused him. Here was a symbol of civilization. Lot observed to Elisha and David, "These Mexican goats are something to behold. They milk 'em from behind."

"Yeah," drawled Elisha, "but I'd like to bask in that Mexican leisure."

They passed through other Mexican villages. In each, the villagers hawked bread, squash, and goat's milk for American pennies. To Lot they chatted in a strange melodious lingo, shrugging and smiling.

Never could Lot forget that memorable evening of 9 October 1846, when he and his fellow soldiers entered Santa Fe. His dust-reddened eyes looked pleasantly upon the streets, stores, houses, and churches. Weary soldiers were gladdened by a friendly greeting from General Alexander Doniphan, a longtime friend of the Mormons and the commander of the post, who ordered a salute of one hundred guns fired in honor of the Mormon Battalion. Lot shared with his weary companions the Mormon respect for General Doniphan. His noble stand during those dark days at Far West, Missouri, had saved the lives of the Prophet and his fellow prisoners, meriting undying gratitude from the Saints. But his military recognition and warm reception of the limping band of Mormon soldiers enshrined himself in Mormon hearts forever. When Colonel Sterling Price with his Missouri cavalry rode into Santa Fe the next day, no gun salute greeted them. After learning of the honor rendered the detestable walking Mormons, he and his men were furious. General Doniphan made certain plenty of ground spaces separated the Mormons from the Missourians.

CHAPTER 7

LEARNING IN SANTA FE

The battalion camped in a field behind the cathedral. Lot had no doubt that Santa Fe was three or four hundred years old. The population was comprised of Mexicans and Indians. Their dress, manners, and habits were strange and novel to Lot. Some of the natives looked on the battalion with suspicion while others appeared friendly. These Americans brought trade for them. The friendly ones came into the army camp daily with red pepper pies, tortillas, pepper pods, and onions as large as saucers to sell to the soldiers. They also carried in wood, corn, beans, meal, apples, grapes, wine, goat's mild, molasses, and cheese. Lot would later recall, "It was the finest cheese I ever saw."

The Mexicans bartered for old shoes, pants, shirts, vests, brass buttons, pocket mirrors, and combs. They preferred these things to money. Lot and his young fellow soldiers treated themselves to good eatables which they hadn't tasted since leaving Council Bluffs.

When the battalion arrived in Santa Fe, John D. Lee and Howard Egan were waiting for them. They had been sent by President Young to get part of the Mormon soldiers' pay to bring back to their families and the Saints now camped on the Nebraska side of the Missouri River. They only carried back a small amount of the soldiers' pay. Captain Jefferson Hunt wrote to President Young: "We are sorry we cannot send you any more money at this time owing to the volunteers getting but one month's and a half pay account for this; but if you should see fit in your wisdom and judgment to send to meet the army in California, we shall be able to send you much more as there will be two months' pay due the first of November."

Lee and Egan brought a number of letters from the families of the battalion. Lot received one from his mother. Her letter seemed to have been written by a shaky hand, and his father inserted a note stating that Lot's mother was not well. Thereafter, Lot's prayers morning and evening were fervent in his dear mother's behalf. To his surprise and delight, Lee also gave him a letter from Lydia Burdick. She wrote, "Keep up good courage. You will make it. God will sustain you. My love and prayers are daily with you." Lydia's letter was never far from Lot's heart. He found scraps of paper and wrote his mother and Lydia assuring them that he was well and liking army life despite long marches and scanty rations.

Having spent much of his youth in Nauvoo with its wide straight streets and lovely brick and frame houses, Lot observed that Santa Fe had never been laid out by plan but had shot up like mushrooms; its streets were crooked and narrow. The majority of the houses were constructed of adobe with flat roofs and contained only one or two rooms. Even the few more elaborate buildings were of an architecture never seen by Lot and his soldier-companions before.

Army headquarters were in the official hacienda—a long, low, flat-roofed structure of many rooms, sturdily built with massive adobe walls. The doors were made of heavy timber and fastened by ornate locks and bolts. Deep narrow recesses formed the windows, giving Lot an impression of peepholes. Before the official hacienda spread a plaza with stone benches and adobe seats. In the evening, the plaza was the center of life and entertainment. Lot and other soldiers were amused as they watched the señoritas walking one way around the square, giggling and stealing glances under their black shawls while their swains, two by two, walked in the opposite direction.

One day, on a brief respite from army duty, Lot and his friends Marshall Hunt, Willard Smith, and James S. Brown, who had arrived with the sick company a day after the first part of the battalion and was still not too well wandered down one of the streets. They were intrigued by the houses of the ruling class which were surrounded by high adobe walls and gates securely locked. Each home had an open patio with flowers and shrubs. They came to an ancient little church built many generations ago by the padres who followed Coronado. In a niche above the door was a statue and a white cross. Within, the wooden seats were old and worn. At the front on the right of the altar, the young men gazed on the image of the Virgin Mary holding the Babe. They hardly suppressed a gasp as they glanced left of the altar at a rude cross with the figure of Christ, a crown of thorns on his head, agony engraved on his face, and blood flowing down his body. "How hideous," whispered Lot.

"I've never seen anything so ghastly before," said Willard.

"I'm glad we Mormons believe in a living Christ," said Marshall.

The padre entered from a back door dressed in a black flowing robe with a rosary about his neck. On his head was a black cap. His voice, though strange to the Mormon soldiers, sounded kindly, and he warmly invited them to kneel in prayer with him.

Sauntering back up the narrow winding street toward the battalion encampment, the friends drew near the market and pleasure center. The peaceful sleepiness the Mormon soldiers had passed through had given way to the raucous noise of the saloons swollen with the trade of Price's Missouri soldiers. Gambling and drinking in the saloons broke the lassitude of the dismal enclosure of the barroom for many of the Missourian soldiers. At times their drunken turbulent behavior had become so obnoxious that some of the soldiers had been jailed under order of General Doniphan.

The guffaws of men's hoarse voices and the shrill cackle of women's laughter were accompanied by the tinkling strings of Spanish guitars. Three drunken Missourians, unconscious from the effects of liquor, had been dumped outside the door of the brothel. The four Mormon soldiers walked past another saloon and came face to face with three of Price's soldiers.

"One side, you d—d Mormons, or we'll smash your faces in," roared a tall, bony Missourian.

"Make way, I say," snarled a second, half-drunken Price man.

Willard gasped, "That's the voice of the Missourian we confronted in Fort Leavenworth with Father's hatchet."

"So it is," replied Lot.

The third Missouri soldier, bearded and large of body, sputtered, "These Mormon nits will soon be lice if we don't squish 'em now," and he took a swing with his fist at Lot who ducked the blow. Before the ruffian could take another punch, Lot belted his big, whiskered jaw with a powerful blow that sent the Missourian sprawling on his backside against the saloon.

The tall, bony Missourian whipped out a knife and lunged toward Lot. Out of the saloon door sprang a large soldier. With a twist of his big hand, he wrenched the knife from the half-drunk Missourian and knocked him to the ground. "Run for your life, boy! I'll handle these pukes without any trouble." That voice! That man!

"Jack Bennington, where did you . . .?"

"If you want to keep your scalp, start galloping! I'll see ya!"

Lot's companions were tearing up a narrow street, and Lot made a beeline after them just as a half-dozen Missourians burst through the saloon door.

Reaching the Mormon Battalion encampment behind the cathedral, almost out of breath after his run from the saloon, Lot was surprised to see officers and their families and soldiers assembled on the parade grounds listening to a large-boned, stubble-bearded colonel who was addressing them. Lot observed, "This man is at least six feet four inches tall. He looks mighty stern. We'll have to hop to his tune." As Lot stepped in line with Company E, Captain Daniel C. Davis whispered hoarsely, "Where have you been? It's our new commander, Colonel Philip St. George Cooke."

Colonel Cooke was making some dry observations about the battalion's march over one thousand miles through an unknown wilderness without road or trail with a wagon train. "This battalion is enlisted too much by families," barked the Colonel. "Some of you are too old, some of you are too young. We are embarrassed with too many women. You women and your families will be sent with the sick men to Pueblo under Captain James Brown. You men are much worn out by traveling on foot and marching from Nauvoo, Illinois. Your clothing is scant, and there is no clothing to issue you. Your mules are utterly broken down. The quartermaster has no funds. But preparations must be pushed and hurried. We must be on our way to California."

"I'm glad we're liberated from that little tyrant, Lieutenant A. J. Smith," exclaimed Private James S. Brown.

Lot agreed but added, "Doc Sanderson will still be with us, and I'm not certain we've bettered ourselves with Cooke. He seems as hard as flint."

Colonel Cooke lined up the battalion for inspection. What a sorry sight! Sanderson and the captains of the five companies scrutinized each soldier. Lot, standing by Willard Smith, was passed by Sanderson and the officers, judged fit to continue the journey to California. Lot observed quietly, "This operation is like a cooper culling stave timber or a butcher separating the lean from the fat sheep."

"I hope Private Brown will pass Sanderson's scrutiny. He's nearing him now," said Willard.

"Look how James S. is bracing himself!" chimed in Lot. "He's looking brave and hardy."

They overheard Doc Sanderson's curt inquiry, "How do you feel?"

Private Brown answered, "First-rate."

The surly doctor looked at him suspiciously and retorted, "You look d——d pale and weak" but passed on. Lot and Willard were greatly relieved when the inspection was over.

Colonel Cooke and Doc Sanderson decided eighty-six ill soldiers would go to Pueblo with the detachment of families under Captain James Brown of Company C. All of Captain Jefferson Hunt's family would be in that company except for Marshall, who would remain with his father and journey to California. His older brother Gilbert, first corporal in Company A, was sent to help convey the sick. As the detachment prepared to depart on October 18, Lot stood by Marshall to bid

Corporal Gilbert and the other members of the Hunt family goodbye. He joined in the family prayer and blessing given the sick baby, Parley, by the father, Jefferson Hunt. Goodbyes and waves of hands marked the leaving of the sick detachment, and it was soon plodding out of Santa Fe.

Lot, anxious to know what kind of commander the battalion had in Colonel Cooke, asked Captain Hunt for his appraisal.

"Lot, Colonel Cooke is a stern disciplinarian and expects every man to do his duty, but he has a sense of humor. He likes young men, and I'm determined to show Colonel Cooke that we Mormons are good soldiers."

Lot soon discovered Colonel Cooke had a peculiar streak in him that led him to test how far the boys of the Mormon Battalion would go in obeying his commands. That evening the colonel ordered Lot to guard a Mexican corral. A United States cavalry unit was camped near the corral. "Private Smith," instructed Colonel Cooke, "if the men come to steal the corral poles, bayonet them." Soon the calvary men walked up and surrounded the corral. While Lot guarded one side, the men hitched up to the corral poles on the other sides and rode off with them.

Soon the Colonel strode over, observed the missing poles, and demanded why Lot had not obeyed orders to bayonet the thieves. The sixteen-year-old private replied, "Sir, if you expect me to bayonet United States troops for taking a pole on the enemy's ground to make a fire, you mistake your man." Lot was placed under guard and expected punishment, but to his great relief, he was released early the next morning, 19 October, to march out of Santa Fe with the Company E, again to the tune of "The Girl I Left Behind Me."

CHAPTER 8

A Month of Horror

L ot, with company E and the entire Mormon Battalion, marched out of Santa Fe the morning of 19 October 1846. Reluctantly, Colonel Cooke permitted the wives of five officers to continue the journey to California. Lieutenant A. J. Smith, who was tolerated by the battalion from Fort Leavenworth to Santa Fe, became the acting commissary of subsistence. General Kearney had appointed three guides—Weaver, Charbonneau, and Lereux— to scout the way for the battalion to travel. Stephen C. Foster, called "Doctor" for some unknown reason, was employed as interpreter. The battalion camped the first night eight miles south of Santa Fe on a stream called Agua Fria (Cold Water). Grass for the animals was short and sparse; the nights were very cold and each soldier had only one blanket to wrap himself in. Lot and his tentmates, now numbering nine since the tents and upright poles had been reduced by two-thirds, used pelts and saddle blankets to try to keep warm.

The road was in heavy sand from the start. The course of the march was southward down the valley of the Rio Grande del Norte. The teams struggled to pull the heavy wagons through the sand. Often twenty men, with the aid of long ropes, were required to help the teams pull the wagons. This was enough to wear out both man and beast. The men, weakened from living on short rations, had to accomplish this heavy burden of tugging wagons, while carrying blankets, knapsacks, and cartridge boxes each containing six rounds of ammunition. They also carried their muskets on their backs. But they struggled valiantly on and on! Each night Lot sank onto the floor of the tent exhausted, aching in every joint, his feet bleeding because of the holes in his shoes. He doubted if he would be fit to trudge another day.

November was a month of horror—destined forever to be a nightmare engraved upon Lot's memory. When the battalion marched out of Santa Fe, the food supply was sufficient for fifty-four days. Colonel Cooke shortened the food rations by three-fourths believing the troops could reach San Diego without undue privation.

The men felt the lash of the colonel's discipline. Captain Hunter of Company B made the first breach of regulations, and he was promptly forced to march in the rear. The men found that their new commander, although strict, was impartial. The officers were expected to obey first as examples for the men. Despite his severity, Colonel Cooke earned the men's respect. Unlike the "little tyrant" Smith, he was fearless and honorable, though curt in speech and inflexibly firm.

Doc Sanderson and his iron spoon remained the battalion's constant burden. His tongue was profanely abusive, and the Mormon soldiers were forced to violate religious principles against their will. Private James Hampton fell sick; and with an oath, Sanderson declared him "well fit for duty." Only hours later Private Hampton was dead. Lot helped dig his grave. Elder Levi Hancock, general authority of the Church, preached the eulogy and composed a poem to commemorate the fall of one of the battalion's valiant soldiers:

> Then we dug a deep grave,
> And we buried him there
> All alone by the grove
> Not a stone to tell where!
> But we piled brush and wood
> And burnt over his grave
> For a cheat to delude
> Both the savage and wolf.
> 'Twas a sad doleful night!
> We by sunrise next day
> When the drums and the fifes
> Had performed reveille—
> When the teams were brought a nigh,
> And our barrage arranged,
> One and all, bid goodbye
> To the grave and the wolves.

One evening in the tent after a grueling day, Lot said, "Did you see the commander perched on the hills above us today. As we groaned pulling the wagon over the sandy hills he sat like a hawk on a fence post shrilling orders at us with the sharpness of—well you know—it is enough to say Colonel Cooke."

"Wading waist deep through the Rio Grande today with all our apparel on was exhausting; but that walking in the sand afterward with shoes full of the d—d stuff, chaffing and galling your flesh without, and the gnawing and grinding of your stomach—plain h—," said James Brown, who was now a tentmate with Lot.

"Little wonder fifty-five of our comrades collapsed yesterday and were sent to Pueblo under Lieutenant Willis to join the other invalid soldiers! We'll all be dead if we have to go through everyday what we went though today," sighed Elisha Smith.

Levi W. Hancock listened with sympathetic feelings to his distressed young tentmates. He, too, had felt the hardships keenly. The patriarch of the battalion, David Pettigrew, was asleep on the tent floor, snoring away his aches after the gruesome march of that November day. "My young brethren," spoke up Levi, "I have composed a song to celebrate our hardships. Join with me in a verse or two. You'll know the old familiar melody we'll sing it to." His tentmates were willing.

> Our hardships reach our rough extremes,
> When valiant men are roped with teams
> Hour after hour, and day by day,
> To wear our strength and life away.
> We see some twenty men or more
> With empty stomachs and footsore,
> Bound to one wagon plodding one
> Through sand, beneath the burning sun.

After each stanza the weary men with spirits somewhat lifted, sang this hopeful refrain:

> How hard it is to wear me out
> Upon this sandy desert route!

As they continued on their way, there were complaints and bitter accusations muttered against Colonel Cooke and the other officers, but the majority of the troops gallantly refused to let hardships embitter their souls or destroy their cheerfulness. At night the shrill but cheerful sounds of the fife, mingled harmoniously with the metallic reeds of the harmonica and bolstered flagging spirits. Wet and cold, Lot and his fellow soldiers continued their march through deep sands, pushing and pulling the wagons until their clothes dried on their sweaty bodies and their shoes were so dry and hard that walking was painful, especially with feet raw and bleeding. Their officers became irritable and often swore at the straggling soldiers, already burdened beyond endurance. Lot's feeling were never so outraged and a desire for vengeance never ran so high, as when an officer, a fellow priesthood holder, cursed at the plodding men who were doing their best. Although Lot cooled down, his physical sufferings were not lessened.

Down the Rio Grande del Norte the weary battalion trudged for 228 miles. General Kearney had abandoned his wagons, leaving orders for the battalion to bring them to California—an added burden! Then the road bore to the southeast, which was not to the liking of Colonel Cooke because it would take him and the Mormon Battalion within hailing distance of General Wool and the United States Army invading Mexico. All of them would lose their trip to California by being led to Mexico and fighting the Mexicans in their own land. The entire battalion was in a pall of gloom. Lot was later to recall his feelings: "All our hopes, conversations, and songs were centered on California. Somewhere on that broad domain we expected to join our families and friends."

Early on the night of November 20, Levi Hancock and David Pettigrew walked quietly into each tent of the battalion boys and whispered, "Brethren, pray fervently this night that Colonel Cooke will change our course to the west and California." The Mormon men joined together in united, fervent prayer.

That night during their prayers, the soldiers heard a crashing noise as though a band of horses were crossing the Rio Grande. The noise caused much alarm because the battalion had heard rumors of the Mexicans revolting. The soldier seized their rifles, thinking the Mexican cavalry were crossing the river to attack them by night. The colonel inquired of the guides and learned that the noise was made by beaver playing in the river. The next morning as the soldiers passed through a grove of cottonwood trees, they observed that many of the trees had been chewed off in long sections by the beavers. Some of the trees were two feet in diameter. A surprisingly large dam had been constructed across the river by the beavers.

On the morning of 21 November the battalion resumed its journey south, marching for two miles. The colonel, discovering the road bearing more southeast than southwest, rose in his saddle and called a halt. With firmness and in the hearing of every member of the battalion, he said, "This is not my course. I was ordered to California, and," he added with an oath, "I will go there or die in the attempt." Turning to the bugler, he ordered, "Blow right!"

Father Pettigrew exclaimed, "God bless the colonel!" The commander looked down on the patriarch and a semblance of a smile crossed his generally expressionless face. A feeling of relief and thanks to God was in every heart. Their prayers were answered.

The battalion recommenced its march west for thirty miles and then northwestward to San Bernardino Rancho. With the change of direction came a marked change in the spirits of the Mormon soldiers. Happily, they sang:

The Upper California, oh that's the land for me!
It lies between the mountains and the great Pacific Sea.
The Saints can be supported there and taste the sweets of liberty.
In Upper California, oh, that's the land for me.

Onward the struggle continued over sandy deserts and through rough mountainous areas in what is now southern Arizona. Hardships were intense. For forty miles they trudged without a drop of water to moisten their parched tongues. The men walked double file in front of the wagons, tramping a trail for the wagon wheels. Lot wrote in his scantily kept diary: "A little brackish water tonight," or "Dry camp tonight," and once "We dipped up some water in our teaspoons." The soldiers staggered as they limped along, many of them looking like death, their eyes sunken beyond recognition. Occasionally one dropped headlong on the desert and was left behind by the stronger ones with a promise to return with water and help. It was the grim survival of the fittest. For Lot, who forced himself forward, it was not human capability but divine power that sustained him. It was a journey of privation and peril endured with patient courage that could never be realized except by those who experienced it.

Colonel Cooke on muleback rode ahead in the hopes of finding water. He wrote in his journal: "A severe trial has been undergone. Forty miles without water." At dark he came to the bottom of a vast lake where there were springs and swamps in the broad area.

To Lot this was the hardest day of the entire journey. His thirst was intense and it didn't seem possible that he could live till morning. Each man of the Battalion looked like death; their mouths black, their eyes sunken. Yet Lot and others struggled on. Their hopes were great. A short distance behind their commander, Colonel Cooke, other officers followed by teams and wagons, and reached the lake bottom. Lot and a few other stronger young soldiers staggered up. The men and beasts quenched their thirst. Lot was selected to ride back with a keg of water on a mule to give a life-saving drink to the men who had fallen exhausted in the sands behind.

Lieutenant George Dykes instructed Lot not to give water to anyone until he reached the last man, and then on his return journey to the springs to stop and give the thirty battalion boys a drink from his keg. Obeying instructions on how to administer the life-saving fluid, he put off three or four men begging for water. "But," he recalled, "I could no longer stand their pleadings. I watered them all and had some left, so I had a drink after I got through a distance of twelve or fourteen miles. I was careful in giving them water, though many drank quite heartily. The Lord surely blessed my little keg of water in a marvelous manner."

For his disobedience to orders, Dykes had Lot tied behind a wagon. He walked in the suffocating dust stirred up by the wagon for miles, which was humiliating to him. However, he never complained, knowing he had performed a service of mercy. This character trait he had developed early in his boyhood, and he repeatedly strengthened it in his later life. His father had told him, "Son take what comes your way and complain not."

Lot was a youth large in stature, over six feet in height, and possessing great stamina and strength. Physically he was capable of trouncing the arrogant Dykes; but as a subordinate in the ranks, he submitted to this indignity without a murmur. (Two days before, two soldiers were tied behind an ox wagon for neglecting to salute Lieutenant Dykes while he was inspecting the night guard.)

When Colonel Cooke discovered Lot stumbling along behind the wagon, he ordered his release and cursed Lieutenant Dykes most severely for this uncalled-for abuse of the sixteen-year-old private.

The battalion soldiers, after a day of rest at the dry lake, toiled on to the summit of the Rocky Mountains, the backbone of the American Continent where the waters were divided, flowing on either side to the Atlantic on the east and the Pacific on the west. Here they found deer, bear, antelope, and small game. This fresh meat was nourishing and rebuilding to the half-starved men. From the lofty eminence reached on the march, the descent was abrupt and steep through the rugged defiles to the valley below. With the pickaxe and crowbar, Lot and his fellow battalion boys cleared the most feasible road down the ravine by chipping out shrubbery and brush and throwing out rocks and boulders. The pack animals hauled much of the baggage down the mountain. Then the men attached long ropes to the wagons and lowered them gradually down the mountainside one by one. Only one broke loose from the men's grasp and plunged to the bottom, smashing into kindling wood and scrap iron.

On the partially level ground below the mountains, the battalion found the climate warmer; and the scrubby ash, sycamore, and black walnut trees had a strange appearance. Even the rocks were different. They were now in Apache country. They passed through a village of Apache Indians whose way of life was alien to the soldiers. Through the efforts of the perceptive guide Charbonneau, half-Indian himself, the battalion obtained fresh mules from the Apaches. The battalion reached the San Pedro River near the present city of El Paso, Texas.

A few miles of travel brought the Mormon soldiers to the deserted San Bernardino Rancho. Once this had been a thriving Spanish settlement possessing many cattle herds. Apache depredations had forced the settlers to flee for their lives and to abandon homes and herds. The thousands of deserted cattle had reverted to primitive wilderness.

While there, Lot and his companions suffered a harrowing experience when ferocious bulls attacked the marching battalion, goring mules, upsetting wagons, and seriously injuring two of the soldiers. The troops had been ordered to march with guns unloaded, but the danger of attack from wild bulls prompted Lot and every battalion member to load their muskets despite the order.

A wild ferocious bull appeared and rushed toward Lot, Willard, and James. Each young man had his gun ready. "Hold," said Lot. "I'll shoot, and we'll have some meat." He felled the creature on the spot, but in a moment it arose and ran away. Willard and James pulled the triggers on their rifles; and amid the roar and flash of the exploded guns, the bull dropped. Some of the battalion fled and others climbed trees. One battalion soldier fell into the deep grass and lay breathless as a running bull passed him. Then he arose and killed the brute. Another maddened bull threw Amos Cox of Company D ten feet in the air and gored his thigh with a horn. A bull came charging where Colonel Cooke and other members of the mounted staff were watching the fight. Corporal Lafayette Frost stood bravely by and watched the running, bellowing bull. Colonel Cooke firmly ordered Frost to load his gun, but the corporal paid no attention to the order. Thinking Frost stupefied with fear, Cooke shouted with an oath for him to run; but this command was little heeded. As the coal black bull was six paces from him, Frost took careful aim and fired; and the beast fell headlong almost at his feet.

The battalion spent two days at the deserted rancho during which time they killed sixty wild bovine. Scaffolds were erected to dry meat which was then stowed in the wagons for the march ahead. Colonel Cooke later told the battalion that the fight with the bulls was the worst skirmish he had ever been in.

The second night in the deserted rancho, Levi W. Hancock, having composed a poem about the bull fight, taught his tentmates to sing a few verses. The last two verses were:

> Whatever cause, we did not know,
> But something prompted them to go,
> When all at once in frantic fight,
> The bulls ran bellowing out of sight.
>
> And when the fearful fight was o'er
> And sound of musket heard no more,
> At least two score of bulls were found
> And two mules dead upon the ground.

As they moved ahead again, Lot was astonished at the springtime appearance of nature. It was December, but the days were warm even to the point of discomfort. The air gave off a lush, fragrant smell which pleased Lot for he felt that the summer coastal plains of California were near. The battalion marched nine miles on the morning of 13 December; then the companies were ordered to halt. Scouts sent ahead had returned with word that the Mexicans were preparing for battle at the Presidio of Tucson, less than thirty miles distant. The Mexican Captain Comaduran was under orders from the governor of Sonora not to allow any United States military force to pass through the town without resistance. The guides informed Colonel Cooke that the choice lay between marching through Tucson or taking a hundred-mile detour over trackless wilderness and mountains. Colonel Cooke decided to march through Tucson.

CHAPTER 9

A PEACEFUL MARCH THROUGH TUCSON

Dr. Foster, the interpreter, was sent to Tucson to try to arrange a peaceful entrance of the battalion into Tucson. He was promptly taken prisoner. The march toward the Mexican town continued. The battalion met the son of Captain Comaduran, who was a corporal, accompanied by three Mexican soldiers. Colonel Cooke put them under guard. From Corporal Comaduran he learned that Foster was being held prisoner by Captain Comaduran. One of the Mexicans was released to return to the presidio with demands for Foster's release. About midnight Foster was brought into camp by two Mexican officers, one of whom was authorized to arrange a special armistice. Colonel Cooke proposed that the Mexicans deliver up a few arms as guarantee of surrender and as a token that the people of Tucson would not fight against the United States.

The next day, while the battalion was still a few miles outside of Tucson, a cavalryman rode up with a note from Captain Comaduran declining the proposition to surrender. The battalion soldiers were ordered to load their muskets and prepare for an encounter with the Mexican garrison. The battalion had not marched far before two Mexicans met them with the news that the garrison at Tucson had fled and had forced most of the inhabitants to leave town. Before proceeding into the town, Colonel Cooke addressed his soldiers:

"We march to Tucson. We come not to make war on Sonora and less still to destroy any important outpost of defense against the Indians, but we will take the straight road before us. But shall I remind you that the American soldier ever shows justice and kindness to the unarmed and unresisting? The property of individuals you will hold sacred. The people of Sonora are not our enemies."

The thirsty, hungry Mormon soldier boys marched through Tucson to the shrill sound of fifes and the rattle of drums. A few aged men and women with some children brought them water and tortillas as tokens of friendship. The battalion camped by a stream a half mile east of Tucson. The battalion purchased wheat, corn, beans, and peas from the remaining Mexicans, and so did individuals. Lot recalled, "We were so near starved we could not wait for this food to be more than half cooked before we ate it."

That night, pickets were placed on duty above Tucson with orders to sound the alarm and awaken the sleeping battalion camp if any body of men more than ten in number appeared. Shortly after midnight, a group of Mexicans put in an appearance. The alarm was given. The bugle sounded at the colonel's quarters. Lieutenant George Oman called excitedly, "Beat the drum, beat that drum! If you can't beat that drum, beat that fife!"

Every man was ordered into line. The drum major, R. D. Sprague, commenced to hit the drum, and George W. Taggart struck a shrill note on his fife. Campfires were replenished, and the suddenly aroused soldiers heard a lively tune. Then came the stern voice of Colonel Cooke, "Cease that music! Douse those lights!" His order was immediately obeyed. The battalion boys stood, some partially clad, ready for action while a detachment was sent to investigate how dangerous the alarm was. Within an hour the detached men returned and reported no danger. The soldiers were allowed to retire again. As Lot and his tentmates settled down on the hard ground with their blankets over them, Levi Hancock expressed the feeling of every battalion boy: "The prophecy of Brother Brigham is being fulfilled that the only fighting we'd have would be with wild beasts."

Though battle with the enemy failed to materialize, battle with thirst, hunger, and disease relentlessly continued. One day's rest at the Tucson encampment was all Colonel Cooke allowed the weary men and mules. Early the next morning, the battalion resumed its march over a ninety-mile desert wilderness to the Gila River. After the first day's march through that miserable stretch of barren waste without water, the men began to straggle along the way. Before the Gila River was reached, the soldiers were scattered over the clay beds and sand strips for twenty miles. The men struggled on and on, day and night, for over two weeks. Scarcity of water and walking in the heat was an agonizing experience. They did not stop at one place more than six hours. Many battalion boys lay down by the wayside without hope that they would live to reach water. Some agonized men rolled a buckshot or two in their mouths, hoping to induce moisture for their parched tongues.

Lieutenant George W. Rosecrans left his staggering and reeling men, rode into the hills in search of water, and found a water hole. Gathering

a few men, including Lot Smith and Christopher Layton, who had sufficient strength to walk to the water, he had them fill canteens. They
brought the refreshing water back to the fallen, parched men. After a
night spent rounding up thirsty stragglers, the battalion resumed its
march.

The battalion reached the green banks of the Gila River in the afternoon, three days before Christmas. As they stumbled into an Indian village, they were surrounded by a thousand friendly Pima Indians. Lot
was impressed by the Pimas. They were a handsome people; peace-
able, happy and carefree, they seemed to have a high degree of affection for each other. The battalion traded buttons cut from their clothing for corn, beans, molasses, and squash.

The hard-driven Mormon soldiers marched on. They camped in a
Maricopa Indian village amid the dome-shaped wickiups of cornstalks
and straw. These natives, like the Pimas, were friendly and proved their
inherent honesty by delivering to Colonel Cooke the mules and goods
Kearney had left with them. Here Colonel Cooke suggested to Captain
Hunt that the Gila country would be a favorable location for the exiled
Mormons.

Lot and his brethren spent Christmas day dragging wagons eighteen
miles along the sandy margin of the Gila River. Lot, young and strong as
he had been, was feeling the rigorous hardships of the march. His face,
like those of the others, was haggard, brooding, and whiskered. The
mules were almost at the end of their endurance. Many of the battalion
were barefoot and their clothes were in tatters. Day after day, Lot
pushed and tugged at the wagons, his faculties dulled. Every mile forward was gained with pain and travail.

Chapter 10

On a Bloodstained Battleground

Three men returning from San Diego met the battalion near the Gila River with the news that the American forces under Commodore Stockston, Lieutenant Colonel John C. Freemont, and General Kearney had fought a decisive battle with the Mexicans at Los Angeles, and the enemy in retreat had surrendered and signed articles of capitulation. The war would be over when the battalion reached the Pacific Ocean, but the battalion was needed to protect the surrendered Californians from the Indians. Colonel Cooke was ordered to move with all speed to Los Angeles. Colonel Cooke weighed the battalion's situation carefully: he could take the stronger men on a forced march to Kearney's assistance or he could keep the battalion together, knowing that the California desert would be treacherous enough for the weakened men and mules alike. He decided they all should stay together.

They followed the windings of the Gila River with stretches of deep sand and miry clay. The exhausted men found little nourishment from the slaughtered, worn-out animals whose bones scarcely contained any flesh. Lot and his tentmates boiled the poor meat and drank the soup, adding two spoonfuls of flour for each man.

Because the mule teams were unable to pull the heavy loads, Colonel Cooke ordered a number of wagon boxes removed and lashed together to make a barge. He loaded it with the battalion's commissary stores. It was the colonel's intention to have the barge tied up to the bank at each night's camp, but his plans went awry when the barge foundered on the sand bar. To re-float the contrivance, part of the precious cargo was removed and left on the river bank. Somehow the unwieldy boat got through the confluence of the Gila and the Colorado carrying its precious cargo of four-hundred pounds of flour.

The country around the two rivers was a picture of desolation to Lot. No vegetation grew beyond the deposited silt, sand, and gravel; bleak mountains, stony hills, and uninviting plains filled his view. The starving mules were tethered in the spiny, rooted, mesquite thickets which contained little bunch grass. Scanty cottonwood boughs provided their night's feed. Lot and thirty-nine other battalion boys were sent to gather the pods of the mesquite shrubs, which were rich in sugar, and returned with fifteen bushels which were spread out on the sand bar to be eaten.

Colonel Cooke had saved some grain and placed it on a blanket to feed his favorite mule. One of the starving freight mules ran up and began to eat the grain. The colonel drove it off several times, but the hungry quadruped always followed him back to the oats. Vexed at the mule and observing Lot as provost guard for the day, he asked, "Private Smith, is your musket loaded?"

"No, sir."

"Then load it and give it to me."

Lot took out a cartridge, bit off the ball end, and spit it onto the ground. Then he rammed the powder and paper down the gun, capped it, and handed the musket to Colonel Cooke. Several of the battalion officers stood looking on. When the mule came back to eat the grain, the Colonel fired into its face. The mule snorted, shook its head, whirled around, and kicked at him; it ran off a few rods but then returned to the grain. This created much amusement on the part of the officers, though Lot had had no intention of any mischievous act. The Colonel handed the musket back to Lot with the remark, "Young man, that gun was not properly loaded. Now, go get me some wire. I'll make a nose bag for my mule, and this d— persistent jackass won't eat his oats."

Lot had started out on the errand when it dawned on him that he did not know what to ask for. He returned to the Colonel and inquired, "Sir, what did you send me for?"

The Colonel in mock rage shouted,"Wire, wire, wire, d— you, sir!"

Lot went in search of wire but was unable to secure any.

"What did you ask for?" demanded Colonel Cooke.

Lot replied in a high voice, "I asked for wire, wire, wire, d— you, sir!"

"That will do, that will do, young man," said the Colonel. "You, you may go to your tent."

A day and a night were spent ferrying men, animals, and provisions across the Colorado in pontoon wagon boxes. Two mules drowned. Colonel Cooke sat on his mule along the bank of the river giving orders.

The boats were in water so deep that the setting poles could not touch the bottom. The Colonel shouted the order, "Try the upper side." The men did but could not touch bottom. The Colonel took off his hat and said, "Goodbye, gentlemen. When you get down to the Gulf of California, give my respects to the folks." He rode off and left them to struggle in the deep water. In a while, he returned and observed that they had reached the opposite shore.

Lot and Christopher Layton had been assisting the preparations for the wagon river crossings. They were both on mules; and when the last ferry departed, they rode up to the river. Christopher had just let down the reins for his mule to drink when Colonel Cooke rode up and said, "Young man, I want you to ride across the river and carry a message for me to Captain Hunt." Private Layton obediently started his mount into the river, which was at that point wider than the Missouri River and just as roily. He barely left the shore when his mule was completely submerged. He stopped the mule. The Colonel hollered out, "Go on, young man. Go on, young man." On a moment's reflection Christopher knew that both he and the mule would be drowned if he proceeded. Colonel Cooke realized the same. Christopher turned his mule out of the river and rode off, saying, as he passed his commanding officer, "Colonel, I'll see you in hell before I drown myself and my mule in that river."

The Colonel's eyes followed him for a moment, and then he asked Lot, "What is that man's name?"

Lot replied, "Christopher Layton, sir."

"Well, he is a saucy fellow."

The march of the battalion from the Colorado River to the Pacific Ocean was over "nature's exhausted region." Much of the dreary trek lay through stretches of sand. The men were again compelled to aid the teams by pulling on ropes tied to the wagons. No water was available except when the men dug deep wells which yielded but little water and that of a poor quality. The suffering of men and beasts was terrifying. The Indians named this region "the hot land." The sun was tropical in the daytime yet cooled to create a winter atmosphere at night. The nearly barefoot soldiers tied their feet up in rawhide and cast-off clothing to protect them from the burning sands. Lot and Marshall Hunt hit upon a novel idea. By stripping the skin from the leg of a dead ox and positioning the natural crook of the knee at their heel, they made the shape of a boot, stitching up the end with sinews. Daniel Tyler, the battalion historian, recorded. "We have found the heaviest sand, hottest days, and coldest nights, with no water and little food." Many of the men were so nearly exhausted from thirst, hunger, and fatigue that they were unable to speak until they reached water or had it brought to them. Those who were strongest when they arrived at Carrisco Creek, a clear running stream which gladdened their eyes, reported to their commanding officer that they had passed many soldiers lying exhausted by the wayside. Dead mules marked the road all the way from the Colorado but no men lost their lives, a tribute to their faith and stamina and to the sagacity of the leaders.

On 17 January all but five wagons were abandoned as well as sixteen suffering mules. A sudden appearance of a San Diego delegation brought hope but when the battalion pushed through a narrow rock canyon which ended in a neck too small for the wagons, despair swept through every heart. At Colonel Cooke's order, out came the crowbars and axes. The Colonel set the example and hewed vigorously with an ax to increase the opening of the narrow crevice. Lot and his brethren struck cutting blows and pried strenuously with picks, crowbars, and axes. But when they tried to get a wagon through, the pass was still too narrow. The sun was but an hour high and seven miles lay before them to the next water. Colonel Cooke had a wagon taken apart and carried through the passage. This experiment proved successful and without too much difficulty the other four wagons were thrust through. The laborious chipping off rock on each ledge of the narrow canyon continued, and the last wagons were pulled through by the mules. The battalion was in California! There was luxuriant grass and water near. Two beeves were butchered and the men ate well. The aching drudgery of the day was salved for Lot when he, with the others, spent the night by a stream of cold water. The next day there was military drill on the prairie.

The battalion scout, Carbonneau, arrived from San Diego with orders for the soldiers to march to Los Angeles and there join General Kearney. The rebellious Mexicans were concentrated at Los Angeles, and the general was marching on the town from the south. Colonel Cooke sent guides ahead to Warner's Ranch for mules and needed supplies.

On 21 January the battalion reached the rancho. Here they enjoyed their first full meal since leaving Council Bluffs—fresh beef (though without salt) and pancakes. It was here that the four hundred pounds of flour salvaged from the barge on the Gila caught up with them. The valley in which the rancho was located was beautiful, shut in by mountains on every side. The stream, Agua Caliente, issuing from rock fissures at a temperature of 170 degrees, sent up clouds of steam for a half mile. The evergreen oak growing plentifully in the valley spread ninety feet into the atmosphere. The imposing sight alone revived the weary battalion boys. Some of the boys found a fiddle that had fared better than its owner, and one of their number struck up the tune of "Leather Britches Full of Stitches." Lot and a number of his companions formed a couple of French Fours and began dancing in water half to their shoe tops. Colonel Cooke caught the sound and inquired what it was. James replied, "Oh nothing, the boys are dancing and making merry over the prospects of getting a little flour." The Colonel shrugged his shoulders and remarked, "I never saw such a d—d set of men before in my life. If they can get some dry clothes and have a little flour they are happy as larks."

While on the march toward Los Angeles, the battalion emerged from a canyon into a valley where they saw a military force forming a line of battle. The advance guard of the battalion slowed, and Colonel Cooke gave the order to prepare for battle. Lot and the other soldiers looked into each other's faces as if to ask. "How do you feel about it? We thought Kearney had vanquished the Mexicans."

Lot voiced that question, speaking to Corporal Arnold Stephens, a Scotsmen. The reply was prompt. "First-rate. I had as lief go into battle as not. If we must die, the sooner the better, for it seems we must be worn till we starve and die anyhow. I do not fear death a particle."

Lot answered, "Arnold, you express my feelings very well." There was no tremor in his heart. Not a single man showed any fear. As the Mormon soldiers drew near the force in their path, dead silence prevailed as each soldier waited for the order to open fire. At that moment, two of the opposite force rode out on horseback, and Colonel Cooke sent two of the interpreters forward to meet them. The interpreters returned shortly and informed the colonel and battalion that the supposed foe was a band of Indians, who the day before had battled the Mexicans in that vicinity and were returning to bury their dead. The Indians' fears were turned to joy when they discovered that the battalion was American soldiers.

A few days later the Mormon Battalion marched over a battleground where General Kearney and his command had found and vanquished the Mexicans. Broken swords, firearms, and dead horses and mules lay on the ground among the graves of the slain. The marching Mormons viewed the still obviously bloodstained soil. Lot's mind recalled the farewell words of President Brigham Young to the battalion: "You are going into an enemy's land at your country's call. If you live your religion, obey and respect your officers, and hold sacred the property of the people among whom you travel, and never take anything but what you pay for, I promise you in the name of Israel's God that not one of you shall fall by the hand of an enemy. Though there will be battles fought in your front and in your rear, on your right hand and on your left, you will not have any fighting to do except with wild beasts." Lot paused to think, "Who on earth dared to make of himself such a promise, under the circumstances and in the name that his promise had been made? From whence came such foresight, if not from the Eternal God, the Creator of the heavens and earth."

CHAPTER 11

GAZING ON THE PACIFIC

With General Kearney's defeat of the Mexicans, the battalion received orders to change their march to San Diego by way of the Mission San Luis del Ray. Reaching this deserted Catholic mission, members of the battalion climbed a bluff and saw the Pacific Ocean. The men cheered in unison—forgetting the trials, hunger, fatigue, and distance from loved ones—and thanked God that their lives had been spared. Daniel Tyler left this momentous moment on record: "The joy, the cheer that filled our souls, none but worn-out pilgrims nearing a haven of rest can imagine. We had talked about and sung of the great Pacific Sea, and we were now upon its very borders, and its beauty far exceeded our most sanguine expectations."

Traveling further, the battalion took up quarters five miles from San Diego; the monotonous hardships of the deserts and the cold atmosphere of the snow-capped mountains were over. January there seemed as pleasant to them as May. Near a gentle brook, the battalion camped. The joyous lark, the spritely blackbird, the melodious bluebird, even the wren, warbled together their evening song. In contrast to these peaceful notes, the fitful roar of the ocean tide and surf upon the rocky shore boomed like thunder.

Lot, with his fellow soldiers, had traveled fourteen hundred miles from Santa Fe in 103 days. An expression of gratitude swelled in the heart of that ragged, barefoot youth. The God he loved and served had mercifully sustained his young servant through all those dreary miles of tribulation. Their destination, as soldiers of the United States, was reached. In another half year Lot would leave California to join his parents and Lydia somewhere in the Rocky Mountains where the martyred prophet Joseph Smith had foretold that the Saints would become a mighty people.

After one day's rest at San Diego, the battalion was ordered back to the deserted Catholic mission at San Louis del Ray. The soldiers obeyed without a murmur. Rumors flew from man to man that General Flores, who had eluded General Kearney and Colonel Freemont with eighteen hundred Californians, lurked in the mountains northwest of the mission waiting to attack. The battalion was supposedly sent there to meet him, although they never saw him nor any California military body.

When the battalion arrived at the mission, they saw for the first time in their lives olive, date, and palm trees growing in the weed-choked gardens. The once stately, arched buildings were dilapidated and neglected. Franciscan friars had walked the cloistered halls and tree-shaded gardens; now Mormon soldiers cooked and slept there. Prayers of faith were again uttered from the mission's precincts to God but in a different manner.

The battalion boys were required to do fatigue duty which entailed cleaning up the place. Cleaning and repairing their quarters was not pleasant; the place was overrun with fleas and filthy vermin. Lot said, "We hunted down the creeping foe and never relented till we routed him. We repeated that attack on the nimble flea and showed him no quarters."

Colonel Cooke then prescribed that no beard be allowed to grow below the tip of the ear, which meant that only moustaches were permitted. Hair also must be clipped even with the tip of the ear. Some of the battalion members had not shaved since the march began and would have preferred not to use scissors or razor until they returned to their families, but the order of the Colonel ruled otherwise. The general cleanup gave the battalion a wholesome appearance.

On 4 February 1847, Colonel Cooke's bulletin, praising the battalion for its heroic march and summarizing the rigors of that march, was read to the Mormon soldiers. They received it with a hearty cheer.

History may be searched in vain for an equal march of infantry. Half of it has been through a wilderness where nothing but savages and wild beasts are found, or deserts where for want of water, there is no living creature. There with almost hopeless labor, we have dug deep wells, which the future traveler will enjoy. Without a guide who has traversed them we have ventured into trackless tablelands where water was not found for several marches. With crowbar and pick and axe in hand, we have worked our way over mountains which seemed to defy aught save the wild goat, and hewed a passage through a chasm of living rock more narrow than our wagons. To bring these first wagons to the Pacific, we have preserved the strength of our mules by herding them over large tracts, which we have laboriously guarded without loss. The garrison of four presidios of Sonora concentrated within the walls of Tucson gave us no pause. We drove them out, with their artillery, but our intercourse with the citizens was unmarked by a single act of injustice. Thus marching half-naked and half-fed and living upon wild animals, we have discovered and made a road of great value to our country.

Arrived at the first settlement of California, after a single day's rest, we cheerfully turned off from the routes to this point of promised repose, to enter upon a campaign, and meet, as we supposed, the approach of an enemy, and this too, without even salt to season our subsistence of fresh meat. Thus volunteers, you have exhibited some high and essential qualities of veterans. But much remains undone. Soon, you will turn your attention to the drill, to system and order, to forms also, which are all necessary for the soldier.

For a month it was drill, drill, and more drill. The teen-age Lot recalled that roll call came at daylight. Sick call was at 7:30 a.m; but through the march and now in California, Lot had never had to go to sick call. Breakfast call came at 8:40 a.m. and drills were at 10 a.m. and 3 p.m., with roll call again at sundown; tattoo came at 8:30 p.m. and taps were at 9 p.m., after which lights must be extinguished. The battalion held religious services on Sunday, presided over by Captain Hunt, Father Pettigrew, or Elder Hancock.

On March 20, Lot's company E and three other companies were ordered to Pueblo de Los Angeles. They took up their march north, traveling over hilly country and passing large herds of cattle and bands of horses. After a four-day march, they arrived at Los Angeles and stacked their arms on Main Street. The natives of the pueblo stood by, reserved and indifferent. Lot was disappointed; the pueblo didn't come up to his expectations. The Spanish city he had pictured to himself had been something to delight the eye. What he saw instead was a squalid town of fewer than five thousand residents, boasting one large Catholic church. The alley-like streets housed a large aggregation of saloons and brothels which the soldiers were warned not to frequent. The houses were typical one-story Spanish adobe roofed with tar, willows, or tile. Earlier American troops had claimed the limited billeting facilities, so the battalion took up quarters in a shaded spot a mile up the San Gabriel River. In early April a petition was circulated and signed by almost all of the battalion members. It requested their discharge on the grounds that peace had been declared and their services could be dispensed with, and the men were needed to aid their families. But the Mormon soldiers were liked and respected so much by the Californians that their re-enlistment was demanded.

The battalion's chief activity was to erect a fort on a mound overlooking Pueblo de Los Angeles and to clean up the town. They cleaned the streets of dogs (they shot the dogs which were an intolerable nuisance) and disposed of rubbish, which was strewn everywhere. Still the army officials, not of the battalion, tolerated more obnoxious annoyances such as drinking, gambling, and lewd conduct. The Sabbath was desecrated with horse racing and bull and cock fighting.

Near the newly built fort, the battalion erected a flagpole from which the glorious Stars and Stripes floated in the breezes from the Pacific Ocean. Lot looked on with pride as the glorious banner waved from the liberty pole but thought that the flag must feel shame at the conduct of some American citizens.

A few of the battalion boys had acquired a knowledge of language and could trade with the natives without an interpreter. Lot and James S. Brown, an eighteen-year-old youth (not related to Captain James Brown who with Lieutenant Luddington took eighty-six men with all the wives in the company up to Pueblo, now in Colorado, to go to winter encampment) were two who had picked up some of the language. They stopped in a cafe for a bite to eat. Besides the landlord, four handsome Spaniards sat at a table. The two Mormon boys sat near them. The Spaniards observed that America was a fine country but said her soldiers were cowards. The two young Mormons, not taking offense, treated this statement as a joke. James replied quietly, "America is a good country and her soldiers are the bravest of the brave."

One of the four stepped into an adjoining room and brought out an American hat cut through by a sharp instrument. "Brave, are you? Ha! Here is one's hat. I killed him in battle. He was a cry baby." Reaching behind him, he flashed toward the two boys a dragoon's sword and two mounted U. S. Pistols. His black eyes flashed as he mimicked the dying soldier crying. "All Americans are cowards!" he taunted.

The anger of Lot and James exploded. Lot demanded, "If the American soldiers were such cowards, why did you Spaniards flee from them on the battlefield?"

Pointing to the Stars and Stripes floating over the fort on the hill, James retorted, "That shows where the brave men are; it is you Californians who are the cowards."

In an instant, the Spaniard snapped a pistol at young Brown which misfired. Quick as a flash, Lot seized a large knife on the table and leaped toward the assailant. The landlord pleaded for reconciliation, while through a door walked six of General Kearney's dragoons. In a moment they had the Spaniard with the pistol disarmed and the other three lined up against the bar.

"Stand back, you Mormon boys. You are religious men, and we are not; we will take all your fights into our own hands," said the corporal. Then to the shaking Spaniards, he shouted, "You shall not impose on these boys. If you ever try it again, we'll slit your cowardly throats." Then to the landlord he said, "Feed these boys while we take these four

greasers by the seat of the breeches and toss them out into the alley."
Suiting actions to words, four of the dragoon men took each Spaniard
by the nape of the neck and the seat of the pants and tossed them out
the door.

As the expiration of the Mormon Battalion's enlistment drew near,
their officers strongly encouraged them to reenlist. The Mormons had
an enviable reputation for industry and frugality. General Kearney
addressed the battalion, expatiating feelingly upon the battalion's arduous journey, their patriotism, and their obedience to order. He sympa-
thized with the Mormons' unsettled circumstances and said he would
represent with pleasure their patriotism to the President of the United
States and in the halls of Congress to give the Mormons the justice
their praiseworthy conduct merited. He ended his complimentary
expression with, "Bonaparte crossed the Alps, but these men have
crossed a continent."

However, the majority of the men preferred returning to their families, even though eighty-one of the younger men, including Lot and
Willard Smith, reenlisted for six months and performed garrison duty
at San Diego.

One day Lot and part of the volunteers, as they were called on reen-
listing, were on the main street of Pueblo de Los Angeles before they
were reassigned to San Diego. A dejected, ragged tramp slouched up to
the Mormon soldiers and addressed them. "I have been waiting several
days to see you Mormons. I deserted the Missouri cavalry and am now
a vagabond. I am in hell. I have been ever since the Haun's Mill tragedy.
I shot the brains out of a boy under the blacksmith's bellows. I obeyed
the orders of the mob leader. Deal with me as you please!"

Lot spoke up and said, "The brother of that boy is here. I will turn
you over to him."

Lot took him over to Willard who recognized the miserable creature
as the Missouri soldier whose hatchet Willard had taken at Fort
Leavenworth. The miserable creature blurted out, "I shot that boy with
a double-barreled shot gun. His pleadings still ring in my ears. Grant
my request; I want to die, and I want you to kill me."

His misery increased when Willard said, "There is a God in the
heavens who will avenge that crime. I will not stain my hands with your
blood." The unfortunate man moved on, his anguish intensifying with
each step.

Shortly after the Missourian had gone, whom should Lot observe
emerging from a saloon but Jack Bennington! Lot called to him and
Jack, recognizing Lot and the other Mormon men, walked to meet
them. Lot and Willard, who knew Jack better than the others, greeted
him.

"Are you Mormon boys still in the army?" inquired Jack."Yes, we reenlisted. Are you?"

"No," replied Jack, "I'm heading north to work for Captain Sutter on the American River. Then I'd like to join up with you Mormon men and be one with you. Elder Hancock told me when I saw him last there might be a chance for me as the killing of my brother was an accident."

Lot was pleased to learn this and expressed the hope they'd meet in the Salt Lake Valley.

CHAPTER 12

Lot Reaches Salt Lake Valley

As the time approached for the company of Mormon volunteers to be mustered out of service, the people of San Diego drafted a petition begging governor Richard B. Mason to use his influence to keep the Mormons in service. The petition was signed by every citizen in town. But Governor Mason's persuasive solicitations failed. Lot and the eighty volunteers were determined to join their people in the Salt Lake Valley.

Captain James Brown of the pueblo detachment had arrived in California with Samuel Brannan, who had brought over two hundred Mormons to the San Francisco Bay on the ship Brooklyn, traveling around Cape Horn. After arriving, Brannan had traveled all the way to Green River in Wyoming, with a few other Mormon men, to persuade Brigham Young to bring the Mormon pioneers to California rather than have them starve to death, as he thought, in the desolate Salt Lake Valley. His efforts to urge the advantage of the Pacific slope as a place of settlement for the Saints were in vain. Upon meeting the returning battalion members in the Sierra Mountains en route to Salt Lake Valley, Brannan told them, "When Brigham Young has fairly tried to settle the arid mountain valleys, he will find that I was right and he was wrong and will move all the Mormons to California."

Captain James Brown had come to San Diego to receive the pay for the pueblo soldiers' services from Governor Mason. From him Lot learned that the first of the pioneers had reached the Salt Lake Valley and intended to settle there. Captain Brown invited Lot to accompany him to the governor. Here Lot heard the governor with unreserved pleasure tell Captain Brown that as a body of men the battalion had religiously respected the rights and feelings of these conquered people.

"Not a word of complaint has reached my ears of a single insult nor an outrage done by a Mormon volunteer. Captain Brown, so high were the opinions entertained of your Mormon boys and of their special fitness that I made strenuous efforts to engage their service for another year. But they refused."

"Governor Mason, can you blame them for refusing? Take this boy, Lot Smith, just turned seventeen years of age. His parents will soon be in Salt Lake Valley, and he is anxious to join them, and they need him to help them make a home." The governor concurred and thanked Lot in person for his services and the type of manhood he exemplified.

Lot and his company of reenlisted soldiers had served eight months when they were mustered out of service. He and a squad of twenty-five men organized themselves for a journey to Salt Lake Valley. Lot purchased a saddle and a three-year-old black stallion, which proved to be the finest horseflesh he ever straddled. He also joined with the others to purchase a band of 135 mules and a wagon.

They traveled the southern route, their wagon being the first to make the journey over this trail. Winter was beginning to settle over the Salt Lake Valley when they arrived. Lot was saddened by the report from Brigham Young that his mother had passed away the winter after his enlistment in the battalion. His father had decided to stay at Council Bluffs. In the spring of 1851, his father was scheduled to reach Salt Lake Valley in a company that included Lydia and her family. Lot was disappointed and impatient, but pleased to know that he'd see his father and his boyhood sweetheart again.

CHAPTER 13

THE SETTLEMENT OF UTAH VALLEY

D irectly south of the great Salt Lake Valley lay one of the most attractive valleys of the great basin. Large hills tapered from the Wasatch range on the east, cut through by the Jordan River in its flow north from Utah Lake to the briny Great Salt Lake. The scenery was strikingly beautiful—broad fields bordered by pastures and mountain streams, the largest one being the Provo River. Mountain peaks bordered the valley on the east, and a sparkling, fresh water lake covered an expansive area on the west. The most majestic of the peaks was known as Mount Timpanogos, towering twelve thousand feet above sea level.

Early Mormon explorers found the climate delightful and well adapted to the growing of fruits and various kinds of grain. Brigham Young, learning of the valley's natural advantages, decided to settle it in typical Mormon style.

The Utah Valley had long been a favorite habitation of many Indians. The tribes who inhabited it were known as Pah Utes, Pah meaning water. These Indians lived mostly on fish caught in the lake and the streams. A goodly number of the Pah Utes were nomadic, lazy, quarrelsome, and deceitful. Yet a few desired to make friends with the Mormons and live among them. Could the Mormons live by them as friends or guard them off as enemies? Only time could tell.

In the last of March 1849, President Brigham Young sent a company of thirty-three families, comprising 150 individuals to settle Utah Valley. They were under the leadership of John S. Higbee, with his brother Isaac and Dimick B. Huntington as counselors. They arrived at the Provo River on 1 April 1849. Before reaching the river, the company was confronted by a Ute Indian named Augatowata. He sprawled down upon the ground and lay across their trail and commanded the Mormons to go no further. Dimick B. Huntington understood the Indian dialects and served as interpreter. He spent an entire hour convincing Augatowata that the Mormons and the Indian people could live together. He told Augatowata that the great white chief had sent them to farm and fish, to instruct the Indians how to cultivate the earth and to learn civilization, and that the Mormons were friends of the redmen, wanting to assist them in every way possible.

The Mormon colonists crossed to the south bank of the Provo River and selected a level site for their fort a mile and a half east of Utah Lake where they could irrigate with river water. The lands were rich and dark; grass suitable for grazing abounded. A heavy growth of large cottonwood and box elder trees lined the river. Four or five miles north of the river a large supply of cedar trees grew. Pine trees were plentiful on the mountainsides and in the canyons.

The three leaders and Captain Jefferson Hunt, who had accompanied the group with his son, Marshall, and Lot Smith, supervised the construction of a fort. In about six weeks the fort was completed, consisting of a stockade twenty-by-thirty rods with opposite sides parallel and equal. Three of the outer walls were composed mostly of cabins built of cottonwood logs in a continuous line. Light was admitted into each cabin through two small windows covered with coarse cloth as the colonists had no glass. Twelve-foot-high pickets were set firmly together deep in the ground to form the south wall and to fill in space between cabins. In the center of the fort was a bastion, or raised platform, fifteen feet high, on which a twelve-pound cannon was placed and fired occasionally to impress upon the natives respect for their new neighbors. A corral was built on the east side of the fort to keep the cattle in during the night.

President Brigham Young instructed the men to finish the fort, keep a constant guard, and not let the Indians inside the fort. They should be cautious and always well prepared for defense. Only Dimick B. Huntington and Alexander Williams were to do any trading with the Indians. President Young further cautioned the Mormon settlers not to be familiar with the Indians. Familiarity would make the Indians bold, impudent, and saucy. "Keep them at a respectful distance all the time," counseled the president, "and they will respect you the more for it."

Lot listened carefully to the counsel sent by President Young and concluded that if trading with the Indians was to be engaged in, it must be through Huntington and Williams who had acquired a good relationship with the Indians. Many years later it was very profitable to him when he was assigned to lead colonization in Arizona. President Young's Indian policy taught Lot that it was better to feed the Indians than to fight them. At the time Lot was at the Utah fort, he was not yet nineteen, but he was over six feet and weighed 190 pounds. He drank no tea, liquor, nor coffee—even when coffee was almost the only liquid the battalion soldiers had to drink. He used no tobacco.

During the colonization of Utah Valley, in spite of all the precautions taken by the leaders to prevent trouble with the Indians, hostilities did break out and became very serious for the new settlers. Unfortunately, when the colony was only four months old, three young men, Richard A. Ivie, H. Rufus Stoddard, and Jerome Zabriskie, rashly accosted an Indian called Old Bishop a short distance from the fort. Ivie asserted that the shirt the Indian was wearing had been stolen from the colony. He tried to take the shirt off the Indian's back, and a scuffle ensued during which the Indian was killed. Fearing the results, the three men weighted the body of the Indian with rocks and sank it in the Provo River.

The Indians, becoming suspicious when Old Bishop failed to show up, started a search and found the body. They were enraged and excited, demanding the colonists deliver up the murderers. The colonists refused. They then insisted on compensation of cattle and horses, but the colonists did nothing to satisfy their demands. Soon afterward the Mormons found their horses and cattle shot with arrows. On numerous occasions persons were shot at when they were a short distance from the fort. The Indians became so belligerent that the settlers prepared for defense. Guards were posted at night, and well-armed horsemen went out to care for the stock during the day. Lot and Marshall were assigned with other young men to herd the cattle.

Open warfare was averted for a few months by a large company of goldseekers en route to California who camped along the outside of the fort. These goldseekers proved a great aid to the colonists. After the California immigrants departed in December, conditions again deteriorated, becoming so critical toward Christmastime that open warfare with the Indians seemed inevitable.

Lot and Marshall had completed their task in helping build the fort. Now Isaac Higbee sent them to Salt Lake City with a report of the serious circumstances the Utah Valley settlers were in. In his report he requested that President Young allow the settlers "the privilege of defending themselves and chastising the Indians." The Church authorities decided to grant the Utah Valley settlers this request. The Nauvoo Legion had been organized in the Salt Lake Valley with Daniel H. Wells as lieutenant general. President Young, however, felt that the federal government should take the lead or at least cooperate in protecting the citizens of the territory.

He therefore reported the serious conditions in Utah Valley to Captain Howard Stansbury of the United States topographical engineers, who, with his associates, had been in Utah since August 1849.

Captain Stansbury, an unbiased non-Mormon, advised that the local militia be called into service as the snow was too deep to get U.S. Troops to Fort Hall. "I did not hesitate to say to them," says Stansbury, "that in my judgment the contemplated expedition against the savage marauders was a measure not only of good policy, but one of absolute necessity and self-preservation."

Stansbury permitted Lieutenant Howland to accompany the expedition as its adjutant and contributed arms, ammunition, tents, and camp equipment for the soldiers. Dr. Blake, of the United States topographical engineers, acted as surgeon for the Mormon militia sent to Utah Valley.

Volunteers rode all night from Salt Lake Valley to Fort Utah to take the Indians unaware and provide an advantageous situation for themselves. The weather was extremely cold, and the foot-deep snow was frozen and crusted. The militia reached the fort on the south side of the Provo River before dawn. Captain Peter W. Connover, commander of the Utah Fort militia, joined with Captain Grant's forces from Salt Lake Valley. Dimick B. Huntington had a long talk with Chief Stick-in-the-Head before the Mormon militia made any attack. A treaty of peace could have been made had it not been for Chief Big Elk and his band of young warriors. They opened fire on the militia, and the battle began. The Indians were strongly entrenched in the willows and timber on the river bottom a mile above the fort. Near the Indian stronghold was a double log house facing the river. James A. Bean and his sons had built this log house but deserted it and took refuge at the fort when the Indians became threatening. This house became the center of action in the fight that ensued. From within this house, the Indians kept a continuous fire upon the fort from the windows and crevices. The firing lasted two days. There was an incessant fusillade between the militia and the Indians behind the river bank enclosure from the house mentioned above. The militia employed artillery against the Indians with little effect as the Indians were under the river bank and most of the balls whizzed harmlessly over them. The Indians made frequent sorties. They thrust their gun barrels through the snow lying deep on the river bank above them, then raised their heads high enough to take aim and discharge broadside at the besiegers. The Indians fought so stubbornly that all efforts to dislodge them were in vain. In the fighting, the son of Isaac Higbee, president of the settlement, was killed, and several of the militia were wounded.

On the afternoon of the second day of fighting, Captain George D. Grant, who had been careful not to expose his men to the enemy, determined to capture the log house at all hazard. He ordered Lieutenant William H. Kimball with fifteen picked men, including Lot Smith, Ephraim K. Hanks, and Robert Burton, to take the log house. They rode up the river bank until they were directly opposite the log house which was a short distance from the river. Lieutenant Kimball ordered the men to charge. Dashing forward through a ravine that hid them from the view of the Indians, the horsemen emerged a few rods from the house. In a volley of fire from the log house, one of the men was wounded, but the other men did not hesitate in their determined charge and the Indians hastily vacated the house and fled to their river entrenchment behind the fallen trees and underbrush.

The first two troopers to enter the house were Lot Smith, spurring his prize stallion straight into the house, and Robert T. Burton. Bullets whizzed past, splintering the logs all around them, but without injuring them. The other men behind the leaders cantered horseback with great speed toward the log house once occupied by the enemy. The Indians recovered from their surprise and poured volleys into the cavalry and the captured building. Half of the horses were instantly killed; their riders escaped into the log enclosure by a miracle. Lieutenant Howland, the adjutant, hit upon an idea of movable battery. They grouped the artillery for more tactical purposes in their deadly assault on the Indians hidden under the river bank. To accomplish this proposed attack they constructed a barricade of planks, pulled from the interior of the log house in the shape of a "V" and placed it upon runners. The outside was camouflaged with brush and boughs. Behind it, Lot and his fellows fired without being exposed as they continually pushed it toward the Indian stronghold. The Indians became thoroughly alarmed at the approach of the strange object; during the darkness of the night, they fled, one party heading in the direction of Rock Canyon, a rough and difficult gorge a few miles east of the fort, and the main party swerving south toward the Spanish Fork River. Later that morning, General Wells pursued the Indians to Rock Canyon. Near the mouth of the canyon were several Indian wickiups. In one of them was the body of Chief Big Elk who had died from wounds received in the battle on the river. He had sworn never to live in peace with the white men. On the approach of the troops, the women and the children fled. Big Elk's wife, a young Indian woman considered to be beautiful and intelligent, attempted to climb up a precipice but slipped and fell, dying instantly.

Another detachment overtook the Indians who had fled south, and during a short encounter with them, dispatched all the warriors but spared the women and children. These were placed in Mormon homes where efforts were made to "civilize" them but with no success. In the spring, they departed and rejoined their Pah Ute tribe. The Utah Valley settlers made a treaty of peace with the Indians who agreed to be friendly and not molest their white neighbors.

CHAPTER 14

LOT MARRIES LYDIA

Lot returned to Salt Lake Valley with General Daniel H. Wells and the other volunteers. Here for the first time Lot became acquainted with the tall, thirty-six-year-old Lieutenant General Daniel H. Wells of the Utah Militia. In height and body proportions, Lot was the general's equal. He observed Wells' soft white skin as he removed his gloves, as well as his auburn hair, blue eyes, large eyes, large mouth and nose, long arms, and large hands. Wells' friendly grasp was like an embrace. Lot felt that warm handclasp and sensed a keen closeness to him which continued in their relationship all the years Lot lived in Utah.

General Wells, Lot discovered, was a gentle-natured man who hated brutality and bloodshed. He felt that the only justification for killing the Indians was in defense of the Mormon settlers' lives. He rode well and looked the part of a general, and Lot rode much of the distance to Salt Lake by his side. Wells took a liking to Lot and encouraged him to join the Utah militia as a regular soldier. As time marched on, these two men, despite the twenty-one years that lay between them, became strongly attached to each other. Lot advanced in rank in the Utah militia until he was promoted to the office of major in the year of 1851. Much of his military astuteness he acquired from the training received from General Daniel H. Wells. Once a week while in Salt Lake Valley, Lot trained with the territorial Militia, called Nauvoo Legion, and became familiar with the astuteness of Well's command and his military tactics. For Lot Smith, 26 September 1851, was one of the most important days in his life. Early in the morning, he rode to the mouth of Emigration Canyon on his prize stallion to meet a company of immigrants who had journeyed from Council Bluffs, Iowa. In that company of thirty-one wagons and 120 persons were his father and his sweetheart, Lydia Burdick. Lot's father was driving two oxen yoked to one of the best wagons his son had seen journey across the plains, and Lydia and her parents traveled with him. Lot noted that his father had aged in the nearly five years of his absence, but his embrace was strong and warm. Each wept tears of joy being together again. Lot was more shy and reserved in his greeting of Lydia who had developed into a lovely young woman. Although her face was sunburned and her calico dress torn in places, she was all Lot had ever dreamed her to be. With a shy smile, Lydia, still sitting on the front seat of the wagon, said sweetly, "How are you, Lot?"

Lot walked nearer the wagon, reached his arms out, and lifted Lydia off the seat, holding her tenderly in his arms. "I'm wonderful now that I've seen you, Lydia. How are you?"

With a twinkle in her eye, the travel-worn girl replied, "Tired after the long journey but happy to be in the valley of Zion; now please let me down."

Later Lot laughed. "I guess I did hold the tired girl in my arms too long."

William Smith came to live with Lot in the small cabin he had built on land acquired from a pioneer in 1847, situated a few yards from the square where the temple would one day rise. Later he built a more roomy dwelling and soon became one with the growing Mormon community in Salt Lake. After a brief courtship, Lot and Lydia were married by General Daniel G. Wells in a civil ceremony. As soon as the Endowment House was built and dedicated, they were sealed for time and eternity. Lot took his beautiful bride to Farmington and there they began a happy life together.

BOOK
2

MORMON
RAIDER

CHAPTER 15

PRELIMINARY TO ACTION

The tenth anniversary of the pioneers' entrance into the Salt Lake Valley was held at Silver Lake near the head of Big Cottonwood Canyon. President Brigham Young, his counselors Heber C. Kimball and Daniel H. Wells (sustained the previous January), and a large body of Saints had spent the day of 23 July 1857 journeying by wagons, carriages, mules and horses from the valley up the narrow canyon road. By nightfall, from actual count, 2,587 persons were camped near the lake. They had traveled in 464 wagons and carriages with 1,028 horses and mules as riding or draft animals. Three hundred and thirty-two oxen and cows were driven up for milk and meat. This anniversary was no small celebration! Five brass bands were on hand to gladden the festivities. There was a military display by the first company of light artillery under command of Adjutant General James Ferguson.

Lot Smith, now twenty-seven years old and an established resident of Farmington for the past seven years, was there with Lydia and their five-year-old son, Samuel. Having been counseled by President Brigham Young to enter plural marriage, Lot had obediently married Jane Walker, the daughter of John Walker and Lydia Holmes Walker, in February 1852 when he was twenty-two years of age. Jane had been born in Vermont and had accompanied her parents to the Salt Lake Valley in 1848 with Heber C. Kimball and company. She was expecting her third child in August, so she remained in Farmington. Lot had also married Julia Smith, a girl of eighteen years, in November 1855. She had also reached the valley in 1848 and, pregnant with her first child, was at home in Farmington. At sunset, a bugle summoned the celebrants to the center of the campground. President Brigham Young recounted the mercies of God to the Saints in the valley in delivering them from their enemies and in making the desert blossom like a rose. Heber C. Kimball prayed for Israel and Israel's enemies and dedicated unto God the ground, the waters, the timber, and even the rocks to be a fit place for those assembled to celebrate the tenth anniversary of the entrance of the pioneers into the valleys of the mountains.

Three spacious boweries with plank floors had been built; and a goodly number of the Saints, including Lot and Lydia, spent the evening in merry dancing.

Lot spoke briefly with President Brigham Young, who inquired after Jane and Julia. The president also expressed his pleasure that Lot had continued with the militia, achieving the rank of major. "Your shrewd capacity in military tactics and fearless mettle in meeting strain and difficulty with fortitude and resilience may soon be called upon for the defense of the kingdom," observed President Young. Lot thanked him for his confidence and modestly said he was ever ready when his services were requested by his leaders.

On 24 July 1857 Lot and Lydia occupied much of the morning reviewing acquaintances with old friends and meeting many new ones. The bands played at intervals throughout the day. Lot enjoyed the martial music much more than did Lydia, who preferred the hymns. Lot and Lydia strolled up on the canyon's tree-clad slope. There they gazed with pride on the Stars and Stripes unfurled on the two highest peaks in sight of the camp, flying from the tops of the two tallest pine trees. As they sat on the high natural incline, Lydia enjoyed the merriment of the Saints below and the music of the bands more because of the softer tones and sounds diminished by the distance.

The bugle summoned them to attend the morning assembly. They arose, brushed the pine needles and twigs from their clothing, and slowly retraced their steps down the hillside trail. They arrived at the gathering in time to sing with over two thousand other voices, "On the Mountain Tops Appearing." George A. Smith, cousin of the martyred Prophet Joseph Smith and a member of the Twelve Apostles, prayed. Each member of the First Presidency gave a message suitable for the celebratory occasion. President Young advised them to attend to prayers at their tents.

A brass howitzer boomed three rounds for each member of the First Presidency, and a few minutes later three rounds were fired for the "Hope of Israel." Captain John W. Young's company of light infantry paraded, and all viewers admired the marchers, fifty boys ranging in age from ten to twelve years. Each one was tastefully uniformed by Governor Young. Lot pressed Lydia's hand. "They are the 'Hope of Israel'; and, in five more years, our Samuel will be one of them."

Near noon, Mayor Abraham O. Smoot of Salt Lake City, Judson Stoddard, and Orrin Porter Rockwell rode into the camp. Smoot and Stoddard, two tired travelers, had driven in a light wagon drawn by swift horses from Kansas City, a distance of a thousand miles in twenty days. On the day of gay festivities, they brought to President Young disturbing news—a United States army numbering twenty-five hundred soldiers had been ordered to Utah by the President of the United States along with a new governor who was anxious to "put down the Mormon rebellion." President Young sent a letter by carrier to General Harney. Under date of 26 August 1857, President Brigham Young said: "I have sent word to General Harney that I wish for peace, and do not want to fight anybody; but he must not come here with a hostile army, and if he undertakes it, we shall prepare to defend ourselves."

Before he was replaced by Johnston, General Harney ordered Captain Steward Van Vliet to ride to Salt Lake City to find a suitable location for the troops near the Mormon capital, far enough away to prevent "an improper association of the troops with the citizens." The soldiers were all to be charged to treat the inhabitants of Utah with kindness and consideration.

It was unfortunate that the purpose of the administration in sending troops to Utah was not known by the Church leaders. Neither did the officers of the army have any clear understanding of their mission. Colonel Alexander, leading the advance division, knew only of its destination; he knew nothing of its purpose, and this is from his own lips.

On September 9, Captain Van Vliet met with leading Church authorities. Although he could present no satisfactory explanation for the purpose of the coming army, he firmly denied the rumors that it was for the conquest and destruction of the Mormon people. On the other hand, Church leaders knew of the uproar in the States against the Mormons because of the false reports of Judge Drummond and others. They were also aware of the talk engaged in by the soldiers. One evening Lot was startled when Jack Bennington greeted him on horseback on a street in Salt Lake City. Bennington was travel-worn, and his horse was gaunt and tired. "Jack, what in heaven's name are you doing here?"

"Lot, I just rode in from the U.S. army. I passed among the soldiers as a lone, gentile traveler and heard plenty. That's why I hurried as fast as horseflesh could carry me to report what I heard to President Young."

He told Brigham Young and other authorities: "The common conversation among the soldiers is that when they get to Utah they'd pick the houses they would live in, and the farms and women would be equally distributed among them. Beauty and Booty were their passwords. Your enemies were to have another Mormon conquest, and all

your farms, houses, wives and daughters were to be the spoils." Other
similar reports were later brought in, so the Mormon leaders knew
what the soldiers were expecting.

Such reports brought bitter memories to the Mormon leaders of
drivings and mobbings in Missouri and their forced expulsion from
Illinois. The authorities found Captain Van Vliet's explanation hardly
reassuring and were not convinced. However, President Young and his
associates liked his gentlemanly manner and depth of character. "We
do not want to fight the United States," said Brigham Young, "but if
they drive us to it, we shall do the best we can, and I will tell you as the
Lord lives, we shall come out conquerors, for we trust in God."

Captain Van Vliet was treated with much courtesy, but the meeting
with President Young and the other Mormon leaders was disappointing
to him. He was informed unmistakably that the Mormons considered
the approaching United States expedition an enemy invading their territory. Therefore, no forage or fuel would be sold to the expedition. In
fact, President Young told Captain Van Vliet firmly that the soldiers
would not be permitted to enter the valley. When the Captain left the
city, he was in sympathy with the Saints and promised to intercede on
his own authority in their behalf. Accompanying him were Orrin Porter
Rockwell, Nathaniel V. Jones, and Stephen Taylor, who escorted the
officer to Ham's Fork, one hundred and fifty miles from Salt Lake City.

The day following Captain Van Vliet's departure to meet and
attempt to stop the incoming supply wagons at Ham's Fork, Governor
Young declared martial law, forbidding all armed forces from entering
the territory and notifying the armed militia to be ready to march to
repel any invasion at a moment's notice. Following the proclamation,
1,250 men were ordered to report at Echo Canyon.

By the last of August, Robert T. Burton and his militiamen met several large government supply trains loaded with provisions for the
army a few miles west of the south pass. Entirely unprotected, the wagons could have been easily burned, but Burton had been ordered not
to interfere with person or property—that adventure would be left for
Lot Smith.

CHAPTER 16

MAJOR LOT SMITH AND HIS RAIDERS

On 3 October 1857, General Wells, John Taylor, George A. Smith, his counselors, and other fighting men, such as Robert T. Burton, Orrin Porter Rockwell, and Lot Smith, held a council of war at Fort Bridger and decided to begin aggressive operations. The Nauvoo Legion, or territorial militia, consisted of almost three thousand men under Lieutenant General Daniel H. Wells. It may have been a citizens' army of undisciplined, ragged men having every variety of weapon, but it was composed of men and boys fighting for homes and families, and they could be "ferocious and deadly."

Orrin Porter Rockwell and a small company of men received these instructions: "Watch for opportunities to set fire to the grass on the windward, so as, if possible, to envelope their trains. Leave no grass before that cannot be burned." Colonel Burton was, with his force, to harass the United States troops in every way possible without risking his men.

Before September 21, Colonel Burton and his command of seventy-five militiamen had arrived at Devil's Gate, where they cached provisions needed for future operations against the United States expedition. The next day his outpost sighted the approaching Fifth Infantry comprising eight companies under command of Colonel Edmund B. Alexander, who had marched out of Fort Leavenworth on July 18. Every movement of the Fifth Infantry was reported by Mormon express riders immediately to General Wells (then at Fort Bridger). Colonel Alexander, extremely uneasy over protecting the supply trains ahead of his troops, ordered several forced marches calculated to get his infantry to Ham's Fork some twenty miles northeast of Fort Bridger. Alexander's soldiers would there await Colonel Philip St. George Cooke's cavalry who were escorting Alfred Cumming, the newly appointed governor of Utah Territory, and his wife. Their chief commander, Colonel Sidney Johnston, would be following Cooke shortly.

General Wells and his counselors in war, George A. Smith and John Taylor, did not want the army so near. Determined to slow the advance, they ordered Porter Rockwell to lead a raid against the approaching soldiers and stampede their mules. With five selected men, he began the first Mormon action against the United States soldiers. Porter knew the terrain over which the army approached very well. It wasn't long until they spied Alexander's encampment at Pacific Springs. About two o'clock on the morning of September 25, Porter and his five raiders moved into action. Each one of them had guns cocked, and large cow bells ready to clang to excite the mules. Behind the army captain's tent, Rockwell's signal burst violently in the air. The entire herd of mules stampeded with a terrific rush. Herders, suddenly awakened, shouted, "Soldiers awake; we are attacked by the d—d Mormons." The half-awake soldiers glimpsed the six raiders galloping through camp, firing revolvers, clanging cow bells, and deafening the ears of the jarred-awake men with war whoops. One drastic thought filled the minds of the herders and soldiers—a whole regiment without a mule to move a wagon!

The day after sending Rockwell out to stampede the mules, General Wells invited Major Lot Smith to take dinner with him and his aids. During the meal, the General looked Lot straight in the eyes and asked, "Major Smith, could you take a few men and turn back the trains that are coming on the road or burn them?"

Lot replied, "I think I can do just what you've told me to do."

His answer pleased General Wells. "President Young told me you are a fearless man and that years ago when you were sixteen years of age and joined the Mormon Battalion, he told you that when the Saints settled in the Rocky Mountains you would perform a great service for them. Lot, I feel this assignment is it. I can furnish you only a few men, but they will be sufficient, for the number will appear many more to the enemy. You'll be furnished no provisions. We expect you to board at the expense of Uncle Sam."

"General Wells, this seems to be an open order; I have no complaints."

The two men shook hands, and the General said, "God bless you!"

Lot was given forty-five men, among whom were Captain Horton D. Haight, Thomas Abbott, and John Vance—officers of the rank and file. Lot requested that Jack Bennington, who had joined the Utah Militia, accompany him. General Wells gave his consent. With his forty-six men, Lot rode eastward all night. As Lot rode by the side of Bennington, he queried him. "Before we met on main street recently, the last time I saw you, Jack, was in California. Now, out of nowhere, you appear in Salt Lake City."

"Lot, after serving my time with the battalion, I returned to Fort Leavenworth. There I worked as a wagon repair man. When I learned that the President of the United States was sending an army to Utah, I saddled my horse and rode pell-mell for the Salt Lake Valley."

"I'm glad you have decided to cast your lot with us and that you are now with Lot, your best friend."

Early the next morning, Lot and his men sighted an ox train headed westward. The wagonmaster of this supply train was a Captain Rankin. Major Smith and his men rode up to the captain and introduced himself: "Captain Rankin, I'm Major Lot Smith of the Utah Militia, and my orders are that you must turn your wagons around and go the other way until you reach the States!"

"By what authority do you issue such orders?" snarled Rankin.

Major Smith pointed to his men and snapped, "The rest of my authority is concealed in the brush by the side of the road, Captain."

Captain Rankin, red-faced with rage, profaned at the orders, but nevertheless shouted to his teamsters to turn their teams and wagons eastward. But as soon as he observed that Major Smith and his men were out of sight, he turned his wagon train westward again. Rankin was met that day by United States troops near the Green River. That night Major Smith and his men camped near the troops.

Major Smith divided his raiding force into two companies, sending Captain Haight with nineteen men to stampede the mules of the tenth regiment and run them off in every direction. With the remaining twenty-three men, Lot galloped for Sandy Fork to intercept wagon trains of supplies approaching from the direction of South Pass. Big Sandy was a tributary to the Green River flowing from the northeast. Lot's scouts reported a train of twenty-six large freight wagons moving down the old "Mormon Trail."

When he and his men neared the wagon encampment much after dark, Lot discovered that the teamsters were awake and noisy with drink. He knew men under the influence of liquor tended to be quarrelsome and ready to fight, so Lot kept his men in ambush, meanwhile sending scouts to "ascertain the exact number and position of the wagons." The scouts returned to report, "Twenty-six wagons in two lines, a short distance apart." When Lot and his men rode into the wagon camp, he discovered with much concern that he had incorrectly interpreted the scouts' report. Instead of twenty-six wagons in two lines a short distance apart, there were two lines a short distance apart with twenty-six wagons in each line. Lot glanced over his shoulder as he rode into the campfire light. He observed his men stretched out for a

long distance behind him and felt sure the bullwhackers would be
deceived by this false appearance of numbers, although he knew now
that the odds were against him.

Lot called for the commander or the wagonmaster. A Mr. Dawson
answered and walked up to Lot astride his mount.

"Mr. Dawson, my men and I are here to burn the wagons of your
train. Your men may get their personal belongings out if they will be
quick about it."

Ashen white, the wagonmaster pled, "For God's sake, don't burn
the trains!"

Coolly Lot replied, "It's for His sake I am going to burn them."

Lot's men disarmed the teamsters, stacking the arms and putting
the men under guard. While Lot and his men were disarming the camp,
a courier rode into camp with a verbal message from Colonel Alexander.
Seeing the teamsters and wagonmaster disarmed and Lot in charge, the
soldier was very frightened. He expected death to follow immediately if
he fell into the hands of the Mormons. He pleaded vigorously for his
life, and Lot, with grim humor, said, "Soldiers' lives are not worth
much; it is only the bullwhackers that can hope to get off easily. Give
your message for I must hear it; and if you lie in repeating it, your life is
forfeit."

The message from Colonel Alexander notified the train captain that
"the Mormons were in the field, that the captain and teamsters must
not go to sleep but keep night guard on their trains, and that four companies of calvary and two pieces of artillery would come over in the
morning to escort the camp."

After the courier delivered the message, he was put under guard
with the teamsters; and Lot asked Dawson, "Is there any powder in the
wagons?"

Dawson consulted the bills of lading and replied, "There are large
quantities of saltpeter and sulphur, and they are almost as dangerous
as powder. Surely you will not burn the wagons; you might be blown to
smithereens."

"Then, Captain Dawson, I'll take no chances with my own men. You
can set the torch to your wagons yourself."

"Oh, Major Smith, I am a sick man, and I do not want to be hurt.
Don't force me to set fire to the wagons," piteously begged Dawson.

"Then I'll excuse you," said Lot. "I'll choose a man who's not afraid
of saltpeter or sulphur: my gentile friend, Jack Bennington. It is proper
for a gentile to spoil the gentiles." Lot grabbed a torch and accompanied Jack. Soon fifty-one wagons were ablaze.

After Lot and his men loaded up with provisions, they rode out
into the night, not stopping until they came to the bluffs of the Green
River. Here Lot and his men had a night's rest, and Lot sent a courier to

report their success to General Wells. Lot recalled, "I told the man selected to carry these dispatches that he must go alone as I could not spare anyone to go with him and that he must look out for the troops, which by this time would be on the alert to capture or kill any of our men they might meet. He said they were welcome to him if they caught him and started away. He got through all right." One early action of these raiders was to burn two important Mormon outposts in eastern Utah, Fort Bridger and Fort Supply, which government forces had expected to occupy. Quartermaster General of the territory, Lewis Robison, applied the torch to Fort Bridger. "It burned very brightly and made a great fire," he afterward reported. Three days later, Fort Supply was burned. The total loss to the Mormons was in excess of $52,000. Rockwell, having carried out his orders with forty men to stampede the government cattle and fire the forage in the army's path, galloped back to Fort Bridger in time to see the last smoldering timber of the old trading post crash to the ground.

Lot did not see the burning of the forts but heard that when Bridger, who had been hired to guide Alexander's troops, saw the ruins a month later, he cursed the Mormons, swearing they were robbers and thieves and claiming they had stolen his fort and then burned it. His memory was pretty short, as two years before, the Mormons had purchased his fort for $4,000 in gold. Lot's courier, finding only ashes at Fort Bridger, dashed on to Cache Cave in Echo Canyon where General Wells had relocated his headquarters.

CHAPTER 17

THE BRAVEST MAN

In the morning following the burning of the Dawson wagons, late in the summer of 1857, Lot and his forty-four bold raiders met another train of supply wagons near the Big Sandy, in a place that has ever since been known as Simpson's Hollow. Riding into the encampment, for the wagons hadn't pulled out for the day, Lot asked for the captain. He was informed that the captain was out after cattle. His men disarmed the bull whacker, while Lot rode out about a half mile to meet the captain, whose name was Simpson. Lot said, "Captain Simpson, I have come on business."

"Business," snorted Simpson. "What's the nature of it?"

"I'll have your pistols first, and then I'll tell you."

"By G-d, sir, no man ever took them yet; and if you think you can without killing me, try it."

The two men rode toward the wagon encampment with their noses as close together as two Scotch terriers and their eyes flashing fire. Lot said to the wagon master, "I admire a brave man, but I don't like to shed blood—unless you insist on my killing you, which will only take a minute, but I don't want to do it." By this time, the two men had reached the wagon train. Simpson, seeing his men under guard, surrendered. "I see you have me at a disadvantage, my men being disarmed."

Lot replied, "I don't need the advantage. What would you do if we should give the men their arms?"

"I'd fight you," snapped Simpson.

"Then," smiled Lot, "we know something about that, too—take up your arms!"

Simpson's teamsters exclaimed, "Not by a d— sight! We came out here to whack bulls, not to fight."

"What do you say to that, Simpson?" Lot asked.

"Damnation," he growled, grinding his teeth violently. "If I'd been here before and they had refused to fight, I would have killed every man of them."

In later years Lot commented, "Captain Simpson was the bravest man I met during the campaign. He was the son-in-law of a large contractor for government freighting. He was terribly exercised over the capture of his wagons."

"What can I do with this bunch of cowardly teamsters left on the plains to starve?" Simpson lamented.

Lot assured him, "We'll give you a wagon loaded with provisions."

"You will give me two," said the captain. "I can tell it by your look!"

Lot told Simpson and his men to take their two wagons and get their personal belongings out of the other wagons quickly for he was in a hurry to go on. Simpson begged Lot not to burn the wagons while he was in sight of them. "It will ruin my reputation as a wagon master."

Lot told Simpson "not to be squeamish. The trains burn very nicely. I have seen them burn before. So be on your way; get yourself out of sight for we haven't time to be ceremonious"

Lot and his fellow raiders supplied themselves with provisions, set the wagons afire, and rode two miles from the Big Sandy to rest. The secluded spot where Lot and his men rested became the scene of the most distressing event which occurred during the entire expedition. While he was reloading his pistol, one of the guards came in from picket duty and one of the United States muskets accidently discharged in the hands of a young soldier, Orson P. Arnold. The heavy ball passed through the boy Arnold's thigh, breaking the bone in a frightful manner, glanced past the side of Philo Dibble's head, and pierced Samuel Bateman's hat, just missing his head and singing his hair.

Lot sprang up and caught the young man as he toppled over on his wounded leg. The jagged points of the bone were protruding, and the blood poured from the awful wound. It appeared as if young Arnold would bleed to death in five minutes. Lot and other men of faith laid their hands on the wounded man's head and blessed him by the power of the priesthood, asking their Heavenly Father to preserve him, for they knew they could not. The bleeding stopped, and Lot proceeded to set the broken bone. The first words young Arnold spoke were, "I shall always be a cripple and will never be able to fight soldiers again." He was carried to Green River on a stretcher. Here he was left in the care of mountaineers until a wagon was sent by General Wells; then the wounded boy was conveyed to Salt Lake City. (Orson Arnold was lame the rest of his days, but he lived an active life and had a useful business career until he died in the spring of 1913.)

While the litter for Arnold was being constructed—the poles had to be procured from a distance—the picket guard came running into camp with the alarming news that two hundred cavalry men were close upon them. Under those trying circumstances, nothing could have caused greater consternation. One of Lot's men suggested they surrender to the cavalry. Lot snapped, "I'll say when to do that!" Another proposed they run, and Lot declared, "I'll kill the man myself if he dare try it." At this alarming hour, Lot made what he termed his first war speech. "Men," he said, "we are not out here on our own choice or on our own business. Our people and their rights are being assailed. It is the Lord's work that we are engaged in, and we are called by him to protect our homes and our religion. If He suffers those troops to come near us, we will trust in Him and whip them no matter about their numbers."

All of Lot's men gathered around him and with admiration exclaimed, "Major Smith, you have spoken right, and we will stand by you wherever you stand!"

Lot felt well paid for stiffening his knees, as he put it, for the poor wounded Orson looked up at him and said, "I knew you wouldn't run away and leave me to die."

When Lot and his men, with the wounded boy, reached the Green River, he sent out scouts to sight the soldiers reported to have been seen. One man ran in and reported that two of the Mormon men were being chased by two soldiers. Lot asked him if the two Mormons were being chased by only two soldiers, and the man replied, "Yes."

"Then I hope they will catch them," said Lot. "I don't want any two men that any other two can chase." All the men laughed. Lot's humor softened the tension they were all under, and the men became more relaxed and alert.

Before leaving the bluffs of Green River, Edwin Booth, the courier Lot had sent to General Wells, returned with Wells' commendation and his encouragement for Lot "to keep a good lookout on your rear as well as ahead, so as not to be surprised by any fresh arrival of troops. Furnish your men and as many others as you conveniently can with supplies of clothing and food from any of the trains when you have a chance. Remain in the rear of the enemy's camp until you receive further orders, not neglecting every opportunity to burn their trains, stampede their stock, and keep them under arms by night surprises so that they will be worn out. May the Lord God of Israel bless you and help you to hedge up the way of our enemies, and cause them to leave our territory." It closed with "Your brother in Christ, Daniel H. Wells."

Shortly after receiving this dispatch in the late fall of 1857, Bill Hickman, who with Porter Rockwell had raided companies independently of the militia, came to Lot and informed him of a large herd of cattle near Mountaineer Fort where Lot's raiders had burned two wagon trains. With Hickman, Lot and his men rode to the place designated. The teamsters of the three trains which had been destroyed were there. They asked Lot if he and his men had come to take the cattle. "We want a few," he told them and rounded up 150 head. Hickman drove them into the Salt Lake Valley. Several of the wagon men accompanied him. They said they had had enough government bullwhacking to last them for the rest of their lives. From his brave friend Simpson, Lot replenished his food supplies, for he had his men spare a few wagons of food supplies. While there he met again a fellow who had been at Fort Bridger when Lot and his men rode off on their raiding exploits. He told Lot that he led a mighty fine lot of men. In questioning him about how many men Lot had led, the man estimated the number to be five hundred. General Wells had told Lot that his numbers would be magnified in the eyes of the enemy.

Lot and his Mormon raiders rode to the Big Sandy to see if other supply wagon trains were on the road. Fortunately, for them and for the raiders, they met no more trains. The success they had experienced "had warmed our blood and the boys were too eager for another encounter," said Lot. President Brigham Young later said to Major Smith, "It was providential for all parties, for if we had burned another train we would have been compelled before the end of the winter to feed the enemy to keep them from starving."

Lot's Mormon raiders succeeded in slowing down the advance of federal troops. The burning of three wagon trains destroyed supplies amounting to 68,832 rations of dried vegetables, 4 tons of bread, 4 tons of coffee, 84 tons of flour, 46 tons of bacon, 3,000 gallons of vinegar, and 7 tons of soap. These supplies would have lasted the entire expedition three months. As we will learn, the Mormon raiders also ran off 1,400 of the 2,000 head of cattle brought by the government expedition. These cattle were driven to Salt Lake Valley and pastured until they were returned to the army the next summer.

Lot and his raiders stopped on Black's Fort not too far from where the vanguard of the United States Army was bivouacked. Early in the morning, after a night's repose on the banks of the Black River, Lot proposed to Mark Bigler, one of his command, that they climb a high peak known as "the lookout" and observe the whereabouts of the army. Within three hundred yards of the summit, they saw some men who appeared to be soldiers. Lot and Mark started a hasty retreat to the camp only to be overtaken by the men. To their happy surprise, they recognized Orrin Porter Rockwell and Thomas Rich with a band of thirty young Mormons. This reinforcement increased Lot's command to eighty men, and he decided to ride up the river to Ham's Fork to see what Colonel Alexander's troops were doing.

CHAPTER 18

LOT AND PORTER ROCKWELL

When the Mormon body of men arrived in sight of the army camp, Lot discovered a large herd of cattle contently grazing on the bottom lands below the army encampment.

"Porter," Lot said, "We'll ride down there and take those cattle."

Porter blustered, "That's just like you, Lot Smith. The stock was left there to trap you. The troops know what a d— fool you are and that you don't know any better than to put your d— foot into their trap. The willows down there are full of artillery. The minute you expose yourself among the stock, they'll blow you and your command higher than Gilderoy's kite"

Lot was unimpressed. "You sit down on your haunches, and I'll ride down and take the cattle myself."

Rockwell replied in a hard tone, "I'll see you burn in limbo before I'll squat here and see you get your stubborn head blown off. I've waited forty years for such a chance, and you want to spoil it." With his field glass, Rockwell surveyed the situation below, but Lot rode his horse down the bluff toward the cattle. Only a third of the men could keep up with him as his horse skidded down the steep descent. Rockwell followed in a terrible rage, swearing at Lot for going so fast, and at the men behind him for being so slow. Rockwell shouted at Lot to wait for him and all the men to catch up, but Lot knew there was no time to wait. Immediate action was imperative to reach the cattle two miles away. By the time Lot and his raiders had reached the cattle, the guard had yoked up teams to three wagons and was driving the herd at double-quick pace for the army camp. While the wagoneers drove the wagons, seven men on horseback moved the cattle rapidly onward. But when Lot and his fellow raiders neared the fleeing government men, the wagoneers leaped from the wagons in fright and the cattle guard froze in their tracks. Lot and the men nearest him unyoked the cattle, and turned their heads the other direction. The Mormon men let out an ear-breaking shout such as the cattle had never heard before, and the frightened steers stampeded so furiously that many of the smaller ones were trampled.

The guards were panic-stricken at the spectacle and looked as pale as death. They anxiously asked Lot if the Mormons were going to drive off the stock, and he replied, "It looks a little as if we would." A number of Lot's raiders were even then in pursuit of the stampeded livestock.

When the guard had seen the Mormon raiders riding recklessly down the bluff much like a band of wild men, they had thrown their guns into the brush hoping no harm would befall them if they were found unarmed. Now when they saw the raiders were only after the cattle, they made a "singular request" to retrieve their arms. Lot gave them permission to do so. Several of the teamsters, upon picking up their guns, fired them to see if they would discharge. Upon hearing the gunshots, fifteen of Lot's men who were following the cattle galloped back, fearful that Porter and Lot had gotten into a fight.

Captain Roupe, the head wagon master, appeared to be as badly scared as the guard. When he recovered a little from his fright, he begged Lot to let him have enough cattle to draw his wagons into camp. Quickly, the Mormon raiders rounded the bellowing cattle into small, easier-to-handle groups and drove them off, leaving the wagon master twenty of the poorest animals to pull his wagons. As Rockwell rode off, he shouted to the wagon master and the others with him, "Roupe! When you get to camp tell Colonel Alexander that we've commenced in earnest. We'll kill every d— soldier unless he turns our men loose! [Three Mormons had been captured by the army.] Do you hear me, Rouge?" Rockwell's features were drawn up into the meanest expression he was capable of forming, and the wagon master had no doubt the he was dead earnest.

With difficulty, Lot kept a straight face. "He was the worst frightened man I ever saw," recalled Lot. "When the guards started for the camp of the government men, they ran the three teams until some of the cattle dropped dead. But they never stopped until they got within the lines."

Spurring their horses onward, Lot and Porter soon overtook their men and the rustled cattle. A rapid count showed that they had procured nearly fourteen hundred head. Dividing the cattle into suitable herds, the raiders drove all night, piloted by Lot and Porter. As the two men rode together, Rockwell enjoyed reflecting on the events of the day and chuckled over his rough remarks to Roupe until his sides ached.

"But what do you have to say about not wanting to rustle the cattle, Porter?" jeered Lot.

"Oh, h—l, man, I don't care to hear anything about that," Porter snapped. "All was well with him that turned out well."

One of the soldiers recalled the harassment of the Mormons, "They set the grass on fire using long torches, and riding horses, so that before pitching tents we always had to fight fire. They destroyed so much of it that the animals had to be driven some distance to get feed. One morning just before daybreak, they rushed through the camp, firing guns and yelling like Indians, driving off all our mules and horses, numbering about one thousand, and before we could get into line they were safely out of reach of our rifles."

Twenty-five years afterward, Lot reflected: "During the whole of the time we were engaged driving off the herd and fitting out the guards, a company of two or three hundred soldiers was visible on the bluff. I have never been able to account for their activity. They appeared to be interested in our movements, but they made no attempt to intercept or stop us; but we were thankful for the herd of good beef cattle, even if we had borrowed them from Uncle Sam."

Rockwell drove the cattle on into the Salt Lake Valley, leaving most of his men with Lot, who regretted his departure very much. Lot said, "I never found many men like him. I think our officers were afraid he and I couldn't get along together. But we could." Lot described their friendship wryly, "I did as I pleased, and he d—d me for it."

CHAPTER 19

LOT MEETS AN ARMY CAPTAIN

After Rockwell left with the cattle for the Salt Lake Valley, Lot and his Mormon raiders rode to Ham's Fork, not far from where the U.S. army had set up camp. The weather had turned cold; the chill in the air and occasional scattered snow flurries were evidence that the season was late, but the army showed no intentions of retreating. The winter of 1848 had set in for sure. Lot wanted to demonstrate to the army that the Mormon raiders were determined the army should go no further; and furthermore, the United States soldiers were too near the Mormon forces to be pleasant for either group. Having most of Rockwell's men and his own command, Lot figured he was strong enough to begin maneuvering through his command. The raiders soon struck the trail of a detachment of troops. Following it, Lot discovered they had unexpectedly ridden very close to a large force of the army. Lot, riding a government mule, led his command over a rough, hilly piece of irregular ground and soon disappeared from the army watch who had spotted his raiders so that they left the impression that Lot's command comprised a greater number of men than they actually were. Lot knew how to spread his forces in such a way as to double their number appeared to the viewer.

The Mormon raiders wanted to stay alert all night, but the cold, disagreeable, atmospheric conditions forced them to wrap up in blankets and attempt to sleep—which in such freezing weather was an impossible undertaking. Mostly the men jumped up and down all night in an effort to keep warm. Fires would have revealed their camp. Suddenly before dawn, they heard the galloping of horse's hooves. The picket rode into camp and reported that soldiers on horseback were galloping past the Mormons' encampment from the east. Lot left the packs and camp equipment with Captain Haight and a squad of men; with the remaining raiders, he followed the troops before predawn light. In a few miles, he and his men overtook the government troops, numbering one hundred, under the command of Captain Randolph B. Marcy. "When they saw us at their heels," recalled Major Smith, "there was some lively scampering for a few moments, and the enemy was brought into line. We halted about forty yards from them, and I advanced and met Captain Marcy about twenty paces from his line of battle."

The army captain introduced himself and surmised, "I suppose you are Captain Smith."

"I am, sir," replied Lot.

"Captain Smith, the soldiers under my command are United States troops," returned Captain Marcy. "What armed force do you command?"

"We are from Utah, sir," was Lot's rejoinder.

Then the cavalry captain asked, "What is your business out here?"

"Watching you," retorted Major Smith. "And what is your business?"

"We are scouting out a way into Utah."

"Nonsense," sneered the Mormon major. "You have left the main road into the valley long ago. It passes through Echo Canyon. I have been that way myself many a time."

The contemptuous manner of Lot's reply brought a smile to Captain Marcy's face. This was the only relaxed expression of the army commander. He remained cool but civil throughout the conversation between himself and Lot. Afterward, Major Smith regretted the rough manner he assumed toward the army officer, who was gentlemanly throughout their interview.

During their verbal exchange, Lot noted the army men knocking the powder down into the barrels of their guns and preparing themselves for an encounter. Lot knew Captain Marcy and his men were out hunting for the Mormon raiders. He had been up Ham's Fork. At the time he was overtaken by the Mormons, he was going downstream but had found the raiders before he had expected. Captain Marcy had no desire to fight the Mormon raiders at the moment. He talked about irrelevant matters but at last said, "I regret the difficulty which seems imminent. The army officers do not want to come to blows with you Mormons."

At this point, Lot retorted, "The government administration seems to want you to. Your coming here puts us in the position of a man holding off the hand that clutched a knife with which to cut his throat. But Captain Marcy, we have a good hold of that arm raised against us and will keep it."

"Captain Smith, I have letters of introduction to parties in Salt Lake, among them one to Mr. John Taylor," persisted the army officer.

"Well," bantered Lot, "you better send them in with someone as you will not be able to go in yourself this winter."

Captain Marcy teasingly asked Lot if he'd take the letters in for him. Lot replied, "The probabilities of my going into Salt Lake are pretty thin. We'll need to go, Captain." Lot rode directly toward the army men, signalling his men to follow. Then they heard the thumping of drums, the shrilling of fifes, bugles sounding, and the shouting of men. To Lot's dismay, he saw they were nearly surrounded by Marcy's cavalry. There was no escape but to go up the steep mountain or to ride straight through the enemy lines. Lot rode his horse into the river but discovered the bank on the other side too steep to clamber up on horseback. Possible escape looked hopeless for a few moments. The troops thundered down on the Mormon raiders as they encircled them.

Leading his men up the river for some distance, Lot sighted a ravine into which they galloped. Lot recalled: "Just as we all got across and had safely clambered up the bank, the cavalry came upon us and commanded us to halt. The boys sent back their compliments, more expressive than elegant, and the main body gave up the chase as we leisurely rode up the hill." Lot dismounted and sat on the hillside holding his reins. Looking across Ham's Fork, he imagined the chagrined feeling Captain Marcy and his men must have acutely experienced having let him and his raiders slip through their fingers.

From another direction, a troop of horsemen rode in upon the Mormon raiders and fired forty shots at them. Luckily for Lot and his men, their range was short, and they overshot their mark except for one bullet which passed through the hat of a raider. Two horses were shot—a gray mare falling near Lot. An exultant shout was heard from the U.S. troops who thought Lot had been hit. Lot was to say, "I felt happy to know that they were mistaken." For an hour Lot and his men had stood face to face with the soldiers without a sign of war, and now for them to deliberately fire upon the raiders "made me rightly mad," said Lot. He was then and there determined "to take a brash with them." If he could have induced the soldiers to come down out of the rocks wherein they had hidden themselves, "we would have whipped them had they been the last troops Uncle Sam had." Lot sent the majority of his men on and kept but twelve with him. "However, even after sending the main command on," wrote Major Smith, "the enemy refused to take up the gauntlet, and we were compelled to ride slowly away without an encounter."

Lot rode to General Daniel H. Well's camp on Black's Fork river. Lot was suffering with a severe cold and was a sick man. He remained at his commander's headquarters a few days, but then was ordered to return to molest the government forces again. He was accompanied by twenty-six men and a baggage wagon.

Brigham Young, Jr., Joseph C. Rich, Howard Spencer, and Stephen Taylor, all still in their teens, volunteered—in fact, insisted—on going with the raiders. General Wells considered them too young for such a dangerous assignment and decided the youngest, Joseph Rich and Howard Spencer, should remain at his camp. Howard had a fever sore on his leg at the time. To show his indifference to hardship and to express his disgust at being kept in camp, he said to his youthful comrades, "Boys, if you want to get out of doing anything, just scratch your leg a little." He rolled up his trouser leg and filled his gaping wound with hot embers from the bonfire. Lot thought young Spencer had the right kind of stuff in him to make a great soldier. And, as Spencer matured in years, he earned the reputation of being a man entirely indifferent to hardship and without fear.

That day Lot and his young men traveled in the coldest weather Utah had ever had. It was October 1857, and winter came early that year. The faces, ears, and feet of the men were nearly frozen. Lot decided to give the teamsters driving the baggage wagon all the blankets to cover them, while he and the mounted men would push on to Colonel Burton's camp on Bear River. Lot was extremely fond of a good horse, and this day he was mounted on a "magnificent horse" who plowed his way through the drifts, breaking through to the Burton camp. When Lot rode up to the welcome campfire, John Woolley told him his nose was frozen. Lot responded, "I don't think so, my nose is too short to get frozen."

Some of the boys' ears were as stiff as sticks and black as coal. Lot bound their frozen ears in snow to thaw them out. When the teamsters arrived, their feet were frozen, though they had had the blankets of twenty-six men to cover them.

Word reached Lot that General Sidney Johnston had arrived at the Ham's Fork army camp, resolved to go on into Salt Lake Valley. Johnston's march to Fort Bridger, a distance of thirty-five miles, was disastrous. "Fifteen days were consumed in this tedious operation. Snowstorms raged, and the thermometer ranged from ten to sixteen degrees below zero."

Lot commented on the snowstorm: "The snow fell and covered the ground to a great depth, but it was not so deep as our chaplain prayed for. He asked for twenty feet. One of our men, a little fearful that his prayer would be answered, wanted to know what would become of him and the rest of us. The chaplain's prayer was the echo of thousands of others offered at the throne of grace by a people whose homes were threatened and who looked to God for deliverance and safety."

When General Johnston and the Utah expedition went into winter quarters on Ham's Fork the last of November, the campaign of Lot and other vigilant Mormon watchmen closed. It ended without the Mormon raiders firing a single shot at the army. Lot was to say, "Had not the Lord fought his people's battles?"

The night after receiving orders for the majority of the men to return home, Lot gathered his men around a blazing campfire. The snow had stopped falling, the weather had moderated, and the Mormon raiders, sipping "Brigham tea" and devouring "borrowed" government beans, meat, and biscuits, recounted their escapades. With the volunteers was William C. Dunbar who, with a resonant singing voice, narrated in song how the Mormon raiders slowed down the advance of the federal troops. To the tune of "Doo Dah Day," Dunbar sang:

> Come brethren, listen to my song,
> Doo dah, doo dah!
> I don't intend to keep you long
> Doo dah, doo dah day!
> About Uncle Sam I'm going to sing
> Doo dah, doo dah!
> He swears destruction on us he'll bring
> Doo dah, doo dah day!
>
> Chorus:
> So let us be on hand
> By Brigham Young to stand
> And if our enemies do appear
> We'll sweep them from the land.
>
> Jonston's Army's on the way
> Doo dah, doo dah!
> The Mormon people for to stay
> Doo dah, doo dah day!
> But the Mormon people all are one
> Doo dah, doo dah!
> United in the gospel plan
> Doo dah, doo dah day!
>
> Chorus
>
> Johnston's army's in a sweat
> Doo dah, doo dah!
> He swears the Mormons he'll upset.
> Doo dah, doo dah day!
> But when he comes, we'll have some fun.
> Doo dah, doo dah!
> To see him and his jinnies run
> Doo dah, doo dah day!

Chorus

There's seven hundred wagons on the way
Doo dah, doo dah!
Their cattle are numerous, too, they say.
Doo dah, doo dah day!
To see them perish t'would be a sin
Doo dah, doo dah!
So we took all they had for bringing them in.
Doo dah, doo dah day!

Chorus

With his cup of "Brigham tea" Dunbar toasted the Mormon leaders.
All the men who had joined in the chorus followed his gesture:

So here's long life to Brigham Young.
Doo dah, doo dah!
And Heber too, for they are one.
Doo dah, doo dah day!
May they and Daniel live to see
Doo dah, doo dah!
This people gain their liberty.
Doo dah, doo dah day!

Chorus

The Mormon boys clapped and guffawed after the song. Lot called
the men to order and closed the campfire gathering with prayer, thank-
ing God for their deliverance from the enemy and petitioning for a safe
journey home. This was a distinguishing characteristic of Major Lot
Smith—to thank his Maker for all blessings with an earnest desire to
have all things done right; nothing short of this would satisfy him.

Lot was soon homeward bound. He vividly recalled: "I had been
keyed up to a higher tension for ten weeks than I ever thought a human
frame could stand. I could ride night and day for weeks and not feel
fatigued; but now upon turning my back upon the scenes of such
absorbing interest, the weariness of months seemed to overpower me,
and I was as weak as a child. This feeling remained, stupefying me, until
we reached President Young's office. He came out to the steps and
spoke about ten words; I did not remember one of them, but they had
the effect to dispel every sense of weakness and weariness. I was ready
that moment to return to the mountains. I would like to know the
words he uttered, though it was not the words but the spirit which dictated them that touched the keynote of my heart. I don't know how
many men could have done it; he could."

Major Lot Smith will ever stand as the one man who did more to
check the army and to prevent its advance into Salt Lake Valley than
any other man except Brigham Young under whose orders he acted.

CHAPTER 20

COLONEL THOMAS L. KANE'S HELP

At Camp Scott, the army's winter bivouac, Johnston and his men were drastically short of rations as a consequence of Major Lot Smith's raids on government supply trains. The colonel ordered Captain Marcy to take a detachment of soldiers across the mountains into New Mexico to bring back mules with supplies.

An irascible federal judge, sent with newly appointed Governor Alfred Cumming, conducted a session of the United States District Court on 30 December 1857. A grand jury brought to the court a bill against twenty Mormons by name and "a multitude of persons (whose names to the Grand Jurors are at present unknown) to the number of one thousand persons or more." The first eight names on the indictment were: Brigham Young, Heber C. Kimball, Daniel H. Wells, John Taylor, George A. Smith, Lot Smith, Porter Rockwell, and William A. Hickman. These and the others listed were charged with treason. They had "wickedly, maliciously, and traitorously levied war against the United States."

During the winter stalemate, the Mormons in the valley prepared for a new and larger onslaught. Word had reached them that over three thousand officers and men had been ordered west in the spring to join Johnston. They were bringing 4,500 supply wagons, five thousand teamsters and blacksmiths, and driving fifty thousand cattle, making a caravan fifty miles in length. The Mormons responded in February by raising a standing army of one thousand mounted riflemen, supported from tithing funds at an estimated cost of a million dollars. Lot was one of its officers. Gunpowder was manufactured by the church public works. The Saints in general were instructed to cache food and other property; and "in case of sudden invasion," burn their homes and fields and "retreat to the mountain fastnesses." Word went abroad for missionaries to hasten home to take up arms in defense of the Saints. On the Sabbath, Monday, and Tuesday following, all Saints fasted and prayed for three days and three nights imploring the Lord's help. President Young's considered judgment was for a peaceful solution. After their fast he told the Saints, "he would exercise faith that the troops should be kept away, and he wished all to do the same."

In Washington, President James Buchanan, hurt by criticism of his impetuous action, was in a mood to compromise his original orders. Thomas L. Kane, a good friend of the Mormons and a former neighbor of the President, solicited permission to arrange with the Mormons a compromise solution. He was given President Buchanan's blessing. Early in January 1858, Colonel Kane left his home in Philadelphia and took ship to Panama under the name of "Dr. Osborne." The ride across the Isthmus of Panama on a new railroad was the most pleasant part of the journey. On the water he was seasick and suffered with headaches which benumbed one of his eyes. When asked why he used a fictitious name, he said, "To see if the Mormons would treat a stranger as kindly as their friend Thomas L. Kane." He found they did.

Arriving in Salt Lake City on February 25, frail and sickly, Kane was entertained by William C. Staines in his palatial home. President Young and other Church leaders met with him. Thomas was discouraged about his physical condition, and President Young comforted him: "Brother Thomas, the Lord sent you here, and he will not let you die. No! You cannot die until your work is done; I want to have your name live with the Saints to all eternity."

Colonel Kane came with a compromise plan which President Young did not accept. Brother Brigham's recommendation was that the colonel go to the army, contact the newly appointed governor, Alfred Cumming, and "do as the Spirit of the Lord led him." With six Mormon men accompanying him, Kane rode through the cold, windswept mountains to Camp Scott. Spring had come to the valleys of the mountains, buttercups and bluebells were in bloom. It was April and the government soldiers were itching to move on into the Salt Lake Valley. When Colonel Kane arrived, having left his escort behind some miles, he was so exhausted he had to be helped from the saddle.

An entire week of interviews with Cumming passed before he succeeded in persuading the newly appointed governor to visit Brigham Young. Albert Sidney Johnston, recently brevetted a brigadier general, wanted nothing less from the Mormons than total submission. His attitude toward Kane remained cool. When he was given President Young's offer to send cattle and flour to the army, then on short rations, the general not only refused but, with an oath, decried the Mormons as rebels and attempted to arrest Kane as a Mormon spy. The slightly built friend of the Mormons was so insulted that he fumed out a challenge to Johnston for a duel. Kane applied to Governor Cumming to act as his second, but Cumming declined to act as his second. Chief Justice Eccles ordered the United States Marshall to arrest all the parties concerned in case another step should be taken in the affair, and the matter was dropped.

After Kane had been three weeks at Camp Scott, from 15 March to 13 April 1858, at Camp Scott, Cumming informed Johnston he was leaving for Salt Lake City without a military escort. The general warned him that the Mormons would poison him. Barely had Kane and Cumming settled themselves in the carriage provided for the 120-mile journey when a mounted patrol led by Porter Rockwell rode seemingly out from nowhere as an official escort sent by Brigham Young. The passage through Echo Canyon had been arranged for nightfall; and for the governor's benefit, the Mormons staged quite a show in the gloomy gulches of Echo Canyon. Massive bonfires shot their flames into the darkness, and Cumming spotted the silhouettes of riflemen against them.

After a group of militiamen had greeted Cumming at one bonfire, they slithered through the brush to the next lighted fire and there presented arms. Every few rods, the governor's carriage was stopped by guards. By the time the party reached the mouth of Weber Canyon, he surmised that three thousand Mormon soldiers manned the fortification in Echo Canyon and that it would be wise for him to advise Johnston to forego an invasion.

Because the snows were deep on the Big Mountain trail, the governor was brought through Weber Canyon; and the party stayed overnight in Farmington. Here Lot Smith welcomed Colonel Kane whom he had met as a boy in Council Bluffs, inviting Kane and Cumming to spend the night at his home, where his wives received them graciously and entertained them well. Lydia administered her home remedy to Colonel Kane before he retired; and the next morning, before he and the governor continued their journey to Salt Lake, he declared he felt much better. Lot didn't inform his visitors that he and his family were soon to vacate their home and flee with the other Saints south if the army were to enter the valley.

On the road from Farmington to Salt Lake City, Kane and Cumming passed wagons loaded with women and children, furniture, clothing, pots, and pans, rolling southward. Before them, herds of cattle, sheep, horses, and even pigs were driven. In the absence of Kane, Brigham Young had "presented the policy which was to remove the grain and the women and the children from the city and the northern settlements, and then, if needs be, burn their homes and lay the country

waste" should the army enter and take possession of the valley. Those
met by the newcomers were some of the thirty thousand leaving their
homes, orchards, and fields at planting time for the barren, windswept
southlands.

President Young and his associates made every effort to convince
the governor that the wild stories about the Mormons were false.
Colonel Kane took him to the Utah library. There he was surprised to
see that the court records had not been burned, as reported by
Drummond. President Young introduced Alfred Cumming as the new
governor, to a Tabernacle congregation. Four thousand Mormons had
assembled. Profound silence prevailed as Cumming told his audience
that he had been appointed governor by the presidency of the United
States with the approval of the Senate. He acknowledged the large
army on the frontiers of the territory but assured the Mormons they
had not been sent to destroy the Utah citizens but to protect them
from the lawless savages. He was sent to enforce the law. But he would
consult with the gentlemen who had been their territorial leaders in
whom the people had confidence. He had nothing to do with their
social or religious views; they had the right to serve God any way they
pleased. He requested the presidency of the Church and the apostles
to counsel with him as a friend. Governor Cumming wrote to the
Secretary of State, apprising him of true conditions in Utah and refuting
falsehoods which had led him to the costly sending of the troops.
Editorials in big eastern papers, foremost among them the *New York
Times*, 28 January 1858, branded the Utah expedition of the army as
Buchanan's blunder. Even General Winfield Scott, the commander-in-
chief of the nation's armed forces, had objections to the Utah
Expedition. President Buchanan subsequently in June 1858 sent a
peace commission to Utah to "pardon" the Mormons. Johnston's army
was allowed to enter the Salt Lake Valley. General Sidney Johnston
ordered the U.S. army to break camp and march to the Salt Lake Valley
13 June 1858 while the peace commission was extending the
President's pardon to the Mormons.

Approximately fifty-five hundred men, soldiers, teamsters, and
camp followers from Camp Scott passed the abandoned and burned
Mormon fortifications and breastworks in Echo Canyon and marched
through Salt Lake City on 26 June 1858. All day long from sunrise till
after sunset, the troops and wagons poured through the abandoned
Mormon capital. The utter silence was broken only by the playing of
the military band, the tramp, tramp, tramp of the regiments, and the
rumbling of the baggage wagons. A few rough-looking men, Lot among
them, were left in the city with orders to set fire to the houses if the
government men tried to occupy them or even remain in the Salt Lake
Valley. Every other man, woman, and child had departed south under

the direction of Brigham Young. Their wagons were loaded with provisions, while sheep, cattle, horses, even pigs were driven in droves before them. They were moving confidently, even cheerfully, deserting their homes—a protest against the interference of secular authority with the freedom of religion. (The popular concept of the Utah Expedition was that it should suppress the "Mormon Marriage System.")

Colonel Philip St. George Cooke, a commander of the cavalry, took off his hat as he passed down the streets in honor of and respect for the Mormon Battalion men he had once commanded. As he passed by the few Mormon men remaining in the city, Major Lot Smith saluted him. The colonel returned the salute.

One soldier characterized the march as being through the deserted streets of a dead city, but the city of Salt Lake was still beautiful. One of the members said it was beautiful, even magnificent. "Every street is bordered by large trees, beneath which and on either side run murmuring brooks with pebbly bottoms. The houses are surrounded by large gardens now green with summer foliage. All the houses are built of adobe nicely washed with some brown earth, the public buildings large and handsomely ornamented surrounded by walls of stone."

The army marched westward miles away from the city limits. They crossed a Jordan River bridge; and after a few days' delay, established permanent quarters in Cedar Valley, forty miles southwest of Salt Lake City, naming the place Camp Floyd.

Four days following the entrance of the army, President Brigham Young made the announcement in Provo to the Saints who had fled their homes, "All who wish to return to their homes in Great Salt Lake City are at liberty to do so." The prophet led the return. Lot drove his wagon to Provo and assisted his own family in their return to Farmington. Within two months, the thirty thousand Mormons were back in their homes in northern Utah.

CHAPTER 21

INTERLUDE: PEACEFUL FAMILY LIFE

Major Lot Smith retired to his home in Farmington and once again took up the pursuit of farming until 1862, when he was placed in command of the Utah volunteers assigned to protect the United States mail route. In October 1861 the telegraph line from the East to Great Salt Lake City was completed, and six months later, President Abraham Lincoln wired President Brigham Young to raise ninety men for three months service "to protect the property of the telegraph and overland mail service, between Forts Bridger and Laramie until United States troops" should reach the Independence Rock where their services were needed. There was commendable dispatch in responding to President Lincoln's call by President Young, and Lot with ninety recruits was on the plains to protect the mail and the telegraph line.

A few years later he was called to serve a mission in Great Britain. After a successful two years of missionary service, he sailed from Liverpool, England, on the Nevada with ninety-three Saints, many of whom he had been instrumental in converting. He and his group arrived in Salt lake City by train in August 1871.

Lot Smith, like every other devout Mormon, believed implicitly in the Bible; and the Bible taught polygamy, which the Mormons preferred to call plural marriage. This form of marriage, as practiced in Bible times, was sanctioned by the Lord. Mormons claimed to be modern Israel; and the Israelites described in the Bible, were polygamists.

Lot, named after one of the polygamists in Bible history, did not condemn polygamy. Not only because it was taught in the Bible, but also because in his eyes a modern prophet named Joseph Smith had had polygamy revealed to him by God with the command to enter again into the practice. What right had any man or any nation to condemn the practice when it was approved by God through his prophets, past and present, who denounced every form of sin?

Mormon polygamy, however, was not a throwback to the biblical system of marriage as practiced by Abraham (uncle of Lot's namesake), Jacob, David, and Solomon. Marriage to the Mormons was for eternity, and there was an equality of the wives and an absence of the concubinage practice. Lot knew and taught that he could not do much good without a wife and that a woman could not wear a celestial crown without a husband.

The practice of plural marriage was a severe mental and moral struggle for Lot even though in Lot's day it was a social institution in Utah. Had his first wife, Lydia, not sustained him and consented to it, he could not have obtained eight wives and sired forty-eight children. She gave her consent for Lot to take other wives because she believed it was right in the sight of God and believed it "to be a principle of the gospel." She once explained, "And if I had not believed that those who obeyed the principles of plural marriage would receive a higher glory in the Eternal World, I would never have tolerated it."

One of the plural wives of Lot Smith was a beautiful nineteen-year-old woman named Laura Burdock, who was sought after by a number of unmarried men. In the mid-sixties Lot felt impressed by the Spirit to propose marriage to her after obtaining permission from her father Bryon Burdock. Lot met this young lady at a gathering in the Social Hall and was immediately attracted to her. When he proposed, Laura inquired, "Do you love me, Major Smith?" Lot replied that he admired and respected her very much, as did his first wife. Lot at the time was only twenty-five years of age. Then Lot added, "You don't love me either, do you?"

Laura said, "I think you are as fine a man, and the most courageous, as I have ever known."

Lot pondered her reply and said, "Love cannot exist without admiration and respect." So Lot took Laura to the Endowment House, just completed and dedicated on the northwest concern of the Temple block, and she became one of his plural wives.

Lot's household in Farmington eventually increased to nine adults—a husband and eight wives. In later years, one of Lot's sons asked his mother, "Mother, did you young women love Father?"

And her reply would have been the same had each of the Major's wives given it: "We learned to love him."

The love of the Smith plural household was the even, quiet, deep kind; their family history is devoid of a single quarrel between husband and any of his wives. Lot assumed the obligation to protect, to provide, and to do everything in his power to insure the happiness of each wife, for each one was equal in his sight. He was also succeeding very well with his farm, cattle, and a dairy herd when he received a call from the Prophet Brigham Young to leave the comforts and prosperity he was beginning to enjoy in Farmington and lead a large group of Saints south to colonize on the Little Colorado in Arizona. The date was February 1876.

BOOK
3

ARIZONA COLONIZER

CHAPTER 22

A FORCEFUL LEADER ON THE LITTLE COLORADO

Shortly after the Mormon pioneers entered the Salt Lake Valley, the Prophet Brigham Young commenced sending out exploratory parties to find new land for the incoming Saints to colonize. Over a period of thirty years, from that July day in 1847 when that modern Moses said, "This is the place," until his death, Brigham Young established a total of 358 settlements in Utah, Idaho, Nevada, Wyoming, Colorado, and Arizona. The settlements on the Little Colorado River were among the last planned and colonized before Brigham Young's death.

The first attempt to colonize within the present limits of Arizona, by the Mormons, failed. In March 1873, President Brigham Young sent an expedition of missionary scouts under the leadership of Norton D. Haight, to explore the Little Colorado area to determine the feasibility of colonization. Missionaries had been sent into the northern parts of Arizona to proselyte the Indians for years before this; foremost was Jacob Hamblin. The route taken by Haight's group was by way of Lee's Ferry where they crossed the Colorado on 11 May. On 22 May, they reached the Little Colorado. To their disappointment there was no green grass and water was scarce. Even along the Little Colorado it was necessary to dig wells in the dry channel. Captain Haight sent an exploring party up the dry bed of the Little Colorado. They were gone eight days and traveled 136 miles up the river. Their report was that the country was barren, with narrow river bottom, and alkaline soil, with no spot suitable in which to settle. In addition, there was danger of attacks from the Apache Indians.

Henry Holmes, one of the vanguard, was especially impressed with the aridity of the land. It was barren and forbidden. The few creeks ran half a mile from their sources. The country was rent with deep chasms and sunk deeper by vast torrents that poured down during the times of heavy rains. The exploring party found petrified trees—one 210 feet long and another that was over five feet across at the butt—this in a land where not a tree or a bush was growing.

On the back track to Salt Lake Valley the company ferried across the Colorado River by 7 July, with 54 wagons, 112 animals, 109 men, 6 women, and a child. President Young directed the missionary scouts of 1873 to remain in Arizona, but his message didn't reach them until they were across the Colorado River and crossing the Buckskin Mountains (now called the Kiabab). The following year President Young ordered another expedition southward. Wiliam H. Soloman, the clerk of the party, under the direction of John L. Blythe, mentions they left Kanab on 6 February 1874, and when they got to Moen Kopi there came to them reports of Navajo uprisings, so most of the party returned to Utah. Jacob Hamblin Amon Tenney, and Ira Hatch, who had taken his family with him, remained at Moen Kopi.

The failure of the Haight expedition and the unsuccessful attempt of the 1874 exploring party did not in any way daunt the Church authorities in their determination to build settlements southward along the Little Colorado. Jacob Hamblin, who had lived among the Indians in northeastern Arizona and southern Utah for twenty years, wrote President Young that it was "for want of faith in the mission they had been called to fill by the Lord" that Haight's exploring mission had failed. After being released from an extensive three year mission to the eastern part of the United States, the fifty-eight-year-old James S. Brown returned to Utah in September 1875. While in New York City he met a childhood friend, Leonard Wines, who, seeing that James had but one leg and learning that the other had been shot off by hunters who mistook him for a bear, was struck with the idea of having an artificial limb made for his handicapped friend. Mr. Wines and some friends raised the necessary amount to pay for it. At a Mr. Nudson's on Broadway, James was measured for an artificial leg and after receiving it, noted in his journal, "Naturally I had a high appreciation of his kindness."

James S. Brown, a Mormon Battalion soldier, a fearless explorer of the western wilderness, and a most successful missionary to the whites and also the Indians, was informed by his family in Salt Lake City on the last day of September 1875, that President Brigham Young wanted to see him. James, in poor health and with an artificial leg could not wait on himself in camp life. When Brother Brigham saw James, he was saddened by his appearance, "Oh, Brother James, if I could see you as I have seen you, strong and active!" he exclaimed. Brother Brown told his Prophet that what the Spirit of the Lord directed through him, he was willing to do to the best of "my ability."

President Young then said: "Bless your soul, the Spirit does and has dictated to me all the time to send you to take charge of a mission in Arizona. You are just the man for it, and if I had sent before, we would have had a mission and settlements there now. I think if we fit you up with a good spring wagon or carriage, and some good brethren to wait on you that you can go." He asked James for a list of the names of good men that would stand by him, and he would call a few such men himself. James Brown put his own name at the head of the list and under it Daniel B. Roson, John C. Thompson, Seth B. Tanner, Morton P. Mortenson, Bengt Jenson, Hans Funk and Ernest Teitjens. To that list President Young added: Andrew L. Gibbons, Luther C. Burnham, Thales H. Haskell, Ira Hatch, Warren M. Johnson, and William H. Gibbons. These God-fearing men were called for the exploring mission at the October General Conference 1875, and set apart on 11 October.

Final instructions were given James S. Brown by letter from the First Presidency: "It will be your duty to found settlements in suitable locations, where the brethren can congregate in cultivating the earth to bring forth substance for the families of the brethren who may feel disposed to join you.

"In the formation of settlements and in all circumstances that may arise on your mission, you will seek the wisdom of the Spirit of the Lord, and be guided by its whisperings in all things from day to day."

When Brother Brown and his fellows reached Kanab on 22 November 1875, he telegraphed President Young, wrote to his family, and arranged with Bishop L. John Nuttal to have their mail sent after them as soon as possible.

They traveled over the Buckskin Mountains down to the House Rock Spring and on to Lee's Fery. After crossing the Colorado they reached Moen Kopi 29 November. "The pleasantest spot we had seen since before arriving at Kanab," noted James. They explored around Moen Kopi. They found a few ponds of water and a good place for a reservoir to catch the spring rains. They built a stove fort there at Moen Kopi twenty by forty feet and twelve feet high. Here in the wild open lands their beef cattle became very wild, so the explorers had to kill them and cure the meat. On 9 December, Brother Brown with J. C. Thompson, Ira Hatch, S. B. Tanner, and L. C. Burnham started on an exploring trip up the Little Colorado River and around the San Francisco Mountains. As they were leaving they were met by Chief Tuba and his wife Telassinimki, who were highly pleased to see their old Mormon friends. Later James ordained Chief Tuba a Priest in the Aaronic Priesthood.

The second day they arrived at the Little Colorado fifty miles above its mouth. The river bottom was a half-mile wide. The group traveled up the wide river bed making careful notes of its course and surrounding territory. Higher up the stream the bottoms widened. They came upon some Mexican sheepherders with four thousand sheep. The water in the river had improved in quantity and quality. The land surrounding the river could be recommended as a place for settlement.

On their return to Moen Kopi the explorers changed their course to the hill country about the San Francisco Mountains. Here they saw plenty of timber, the finest they had seen. However they encountered a "terrific snow storm." Their progress was slow in the deep snow. James notes "we were thankful to reach the river on 28 December and Moen Kopi on 29 December." After a brief consultation, the group decided that James Brown should return to Salt Lake City and report to President Young their observations and explorations. About the time he was to start, the bandaging of his artificial leg gave way, but Thales Haskell repaired it. J. C. Thompson and W. H. Gibbons accompanied James to Kanab.

From Kanab he was conveyed by bishops of different villages he passed through from one village to the next. Above Monroe he was taken by a brother to the Railroad station. A ticket sent by President Young was awaiting him. He arrived in Salt Lake City at 6 p.m. 14 January 1876. James S. Brown wrote: "If I had been President Young's own son, he could not have received me more cordially than he did when I reached his office." Brown's family were overjoyed to see him.

Why were the Mormons sent by Brigham Young to settle along the Little Colorado? In his instructions to the leaders, one of whom was Lot Smith, he gave three major objectives: (1) to make homes for the Saints, (2) to make acquaintance with the Indians, and (3) to found United Orders and to make them work. The Saints who responded did so with the firm conviction that their call had come from a prophet of God.

To gain information about the land and water resources, President Young had sent missionary scouts into northeastern Arizona. Horton Haight had led one exploring party of seasoned pioneers in 1873.

President Young and his counselors had anticipated a favorable report from James Brown, and quick action was immediate. They organized four companies of fifty men and their families. Lot Smith captained one of them. The other three captains were: William C. Allen, Jesse O. Ballenger, and George Lake. In calling Lot to lead one of the companies, President Young said in the hearing of many, "I will send a man who will stay there." Lot Smith was a man of proven abilities. While he was appointed captain of only one of the four companies, it was known that he was to be the first among equals. To the leaders of the four companies, three major objectives for the colonization on the Little Colorado River were stressed by the First Presidency. In private, Brigham Young said to him, "You are hereby appointed to take charge of the mission about to go south and southeast of the Colorado River. It is your duty to found settlements in suitable locations for Latter-day Saints to build homes, to reclaim the Indians, and build up the United Order."

The 200 missionaries were called from many parts of Utah Territory to go and settle the Little Colorado. There was no formal gathering of the companies. The assembling point was Kanab. Then there was assemblage of groups of about ten families each, without reference to companies.

The colonizers thoroughly packed and equipped their wagons with enough supplies to last for a year after they reached their destination. During their travels south, Lot and all his family slept in their several wagons and cooked over an open fire. Some of the pioneers took along special stocks of food—one had mixed sacks of flour with cream of tarter and salt ready for biscuit baking. Another bound a hive of bees to the end gate of his last wagon so he would have honey.

The distance to the Little Colorado traveled by Lot and his fellow colonizers was six hundred miles. Half the journey was through Mormon settlements, Kanab being the last outpost and assembling point. Here the colonizers were organized under each of the four captains. From Kanab south the road was poor, when there was any road at all. Pulling the wagons over the Buckskin Mountains was strenuous. The back wagon wheels had to be chained to go down the mountainside to Houserock Valley and Springs. In the valley, the road turned northeast around the Vermillion Cliffs to the Colorado River.

The most dangerous phase of the journey was crossing the Colorado River. Lee's Ferry was the site where most of the colonists crossed. John D. Lee, who had participated in the Mountain Meadow Massacre in 1857 had taken refuge there. Lee had explored the Colorado River and was in seclusion among the Hava-Supei Indians in the remote Cataract Canyon. When he came he brought seeds and pits from which sprang the Indian orchards. Lee located at the mouth of Paria, built a log cabin, and acquired ferry rights that had been possessed by the Church. In this seldom-visited spot Lee prepared a ferry strong enough to carry teams and wagons to the opposite side, though his ferry was lost a few months afterwards. In June 1874 an Indian trading post was established at the ferry, and in the fall of that year Lee departed from the river. John L. Blythe built a second ferry capable of carrying two loaded wagons and teams. This was the ferry utilized by Lot Smith and fellow pioneers. After reaching the Arizona side of the river, they had to make a two mile pull up a rocky, narrow, steep dugway with doubled teams.

After Lot and his family had pulled their wagons up Lee's Hill, they camped on the Arizona side of the Colorado. Knowing it would be a considerable distance to the next watering hole, the next morning Lot and his sons took the horses back to the Colorado River to let them drink. Surprising Lot and his boys, the horses ran to the river, plunged into the roaring waters, and swam across to the other side, leaving their attendants alone. One of Lot's sons, who wasn't pleased with having to leave Farmington, said indignantly, "Father, even the horses don't want to go to the forsaken country of the Little Colorado."

Lot smiled as he answered, "It surely looks that way, doesn't it?"

When the horses reached the Utah side of the river, the ferryman stopped them, tied them up, and rowed across the river to fetch Lot and his boys. With difficulty, they finally got the horses back to the Arizona side of the Colorado.

Few, if any, of the colonists called to settle the Little Colorado had any personal knowledge of the country to which they were going, and Lot Smith was among them. But the direction to travel from the ferry had been given them. Lot and the other pioneers with him turned south to Bitter Springs; then they crossed Cedar Ridge to the Gap and went on to Moen Kopi. They arrived at the Little Colorado a few miles above present day Cameron. Remaining on the north side of the river until six miles above the Grand Falls, they crossed the river and traveled to the Sunset Crossing east of the modern town of Winslow. The farther they traveled, the less inviting the scenery became. "This is the most desert-looking place I ever saw. There ain't no fit place for a human being to dwell upon," lamented one of Lot's wives.

Lot tried to reassure her. "I don't know whether it makes any difference whether the country is barren or fruitful if the Lord has a work for us to do in it."

One of Lot's older sons joined in, "Father, this land has been forsaken by the Lord; how could he have work for anyone to do in it?"

"That Little Colorado is a nasty, muddy stream," chimed in another member of the Smith family. "I tried to moisten my lips, and it tasted like salt; and the mud in it gritted my teeth."

"We'll camp here for the night, son, and fill our kettle with the river water; by morning the mud will have settled to the bottom, and we'll have clear drinking water," said Lot trying to cheer up his family. But the next morning only one inch of clear water was found on top of the seven gallon kettle.

Little did Lot and his fellow pioneers then know that the Little Colorado was a river of extremes; either there was too much water or not enough. Like a running stream of reddish-colored mud, there would be plenty in March and April; but in the summer when irrigation was needed most, the flow of the water would be low. The Little Colorado is a treacherous stream at best, with a broad channel of water that cuts through the alluvial country which melts like sugar or salt at the touch of water. These pioneers would experience the discouraging task of building dam after dam, only to see each one washed away by the floods. After each dam built by strenuous labor, a prayer would fervently be offered: "O Lord, we pray that this dam may stand, if it be Thy will—if not, let Thy will be done." And it generally washed away.

To the new settlers from Utah, everything appeared as a desert—large open country, dreary and forbidding, rent by deep chasms which were made deeper by vast torrents of water that poured down them during heavy rains. However, beyond the meandering riverbed, grass grew during March of the year, and beyond was a belt of large, thrifty, cottonwood forests a mile wide for fifty miles. (But what could the pioneers make out of the soft, crooked cottonwood?) Driftwood was plentiful along the river edge. "Wherever we settle it won't be too far away from this abundant supply of wood and early spring grazing for the cattle," commented Lot to members of his company.

"We can make a fire, at least, can't we?" asked Lot, Jr.

"We'll make more than fire here, son," confidently said his father. They continued their travel eastward up the Little Colorado, over sand hills and up washes.

The missionary settlers, as they called themselves, arrived at a spot some five miles from the present site of Joseph City on 24 March 1876. Here, waiting for them, was James S. Brown who had established his headquarters at Moen Kopi but had ridden on to the Little Colorado to guide the four captains and their companies of fifty men and families each to the places selected for their settlements. After supper, Brown invited Lot Smith and the other leaders to his camp to discuss what would be done by way of settling the area. Brown presented to them the letter of instructions that President Brigham Young had given him which also contained his appointment as president of the mission. There apparently was a misunderstanding as to which one had been appointed by President Brigham Young to preside over the colonizing mission. Lot and the other captains opposed Brown's presidency of the mission and refused to give him their support. Feelings were raw and the atmosphere very unpleasant. The meeting was dismissed and all retired to ponder the situation. The next day Brown invited Lot to walk with him away from the camp. When James asked Lot what he intended to do, the once Mormon raider retorted, "I am going ahead independent of you."

"Lot Smith," said Brown, "in our youth we were battalion soldiers together, and you were right congenial then to get along with, but now you have trampled on my God-given right through President Young who has appointed me to preside over the Arizona Mission. If you persist in doing wrong, you must bear the responsibility."

"James, President Young appointed me to be the presiding officer down here, and I shall act as such," counter-argued Lot.

With that defiant reply, Brown decided to return at once to Moen Kopi. He and his party bade goodbye to the newcomers and departed.

The confrontation between Lot and James was a very unfortunate beginning for this colonial venture, which should have been dominated by the spirit of brotherly love. Before the end of the year, a letter arrived for Lot Smith from Brigham Young wherein he was given "general oversight of the affairs of the camp." James S. Brown was informed that his commission given him by President Young did not include "the four companies of fity men and families that were afterward called." The decision of where the four companies were to settle was left in the hands of the captains. Lot Smith took his company thirteen miles downriver and settled on the northeast side of the Little Colorado two miles below the Sunset Crossing. Allen and Lake continued up the river twenty miles to a suitable place to begin a settlement about five miles east of the present site of Joseph City. Ballenger's company located four miles southwest of Sunset Crossing near the site of the present city of Winslow. The location was on low ground among some cotton-wood trees. The Indians warned Lot that if the Mormons intended to live there, "you had better fix scaffolding in the trees, for the river gets mad sometimes."

Lot and his fellow explorers noted that the only timber of consequence along the Little Colorado was cottonwood. It was not suitable for logs; but it was the only wood available, so they used it. They built a fort two hundred feet square, with rocky walls seven feet high. Inside were thirty-six dwelling cabins made of cottonwood logs, each fifteen by thirteen feet. Lot needed a number of these huts for his own family. On the north side, they built a dining hall eighty by forty feet with two rows of tables, enough to seat more than 150 persons. A kitchen and bakehouse adjoined it. Later they constructed twelve other dwelling cabins plus a cellar and storehouse. Two good wells were dug; and though the water was bad-tasting, the settlers got used to it.

Some of the new settlers were skeptical about the land's productivity, but they plowed the land, built dams, and made canals to bring the water onto their planted acreage anyway. Within two years, they had two hundred acres of wheat, one hundred acres of corn, fifteen acres of sugar cane, fifteen acres of alfalfa, and five acres of vegetables. But the most favorable promise of the Little Colorado country, with its wide-open, grassy ranges, was stock-raising. Along with their crops, the Sunset settlements had sixty-five brood mares, thirty yearlings, twenty-one young colts, and fifteen horses. Many of these were used to take care of 300 oxen, 160 milch cows, 257 dry stock, 1,200 sheep, and 500 lambs.

The first fall, Lot, with others, explored the higher elevations south and east of the present city of Flagstaff and laid claims to Pleasant Valley, which they called Mormon Lake. Lot and his fellow explorers rode into the Pleasant Valley. "This is so beautiful, brethren" exclaimed Lot, "that we could call it a park."

"It is a park—park pleasant," agreed Joseph Rogers. It contained about 4,000 acres, without stick, stone, or brush with soil as black and rich as the Missouri bottoms. Far to the west was a fresh water lake where Lot and his group refreshed themselves and their mounts. The valley was shielded on the north by the San Francisco Mountains and hills, and open to the south, surrounded on every side by an immense forest of giant pine timber. There was no underbrush and the trees stood from six inches to four feet in diameter and towered to the height of fifty to one hundred and fifty feet. A heavy growth of nutritious bunch grass covered the ground. "An excellent range for horses, cattle, and sheep," the brethren agreed.

In a short time Lot and his fellow colonizers turned Pleasant Valley into a paradise for stock and formed a big communal dairy. It was owned and operated jointly by Sunset and the other three colonies. The dairy became their most profitable venture. Besides making cheese and butter, the Arizona pioneers raised hogs on the by-products of the dairy. In Pleasant Valley the colonists grew an abundance of potatoes without irrigation. Lot Smith established a dairy in September 1878, sixty miles west of Sunset. In that year 48 men and 41 women from Sunset and the other settlements were at the dairy, caring for 115 cows and the making of butter and cheese. Three good log houses were built. Seven miles south of Pleasant Valley, Lot took the lead in building a saw mill. The mill in 1876 was taken down by Warren R. Tenney who re-erected it in the pine woods near Mormon Lake. He was soon turning out 100,00 feet of boards. This new site was named Millville.

To Lot Smith, Warren Tenney, and other stalwarts sent to settle the Little Colorado, the Lord was prospering them richly and they praised his name for being sent on such a mission. But there were others, "the weak kneed," who, when the first dams washed out in July of the first year, with their families returned to Utah, supposedly just for the winter and to bring back supplies. Many of them never returned. By 1879 Lot left on record that the Sunset settlement consisted of 25 families—24 men, 30 women, and 66 children—a total of 120 souls, who like their leaders, would stay on their mission until released by the Lord who sent them.

CHAPTER 23

THE UNITED ORDER

In the winter of 1874, President Brigham Young inaugurated the United Order, after the pattern of the law of consecration and stewardship initiated by the Prophet Joseph Smith in 1831. The movement intended to lead the Saints through a complete consecration of their earthly possessions, to a closer union with more purpose and spiritual unity. Uniting the Saints in their material interest was to secure a higher spiritual union among them, These purposes were revealed in the remarks of President Young when he introduced the program for the consideration of those in attendance to the 44th annual conference of the Church. Said the Prophet Brigham:

"And when the question is asked—'Whose is this?' the earnings and savings of this community, organized to sustain and promote the kingdom of God on the earth, the answer will be: 'It is ours, and we are the Lords, and all that we have belongs to him. He has placed this in our possession, for our improvement and to see what we will do with it, and whether we devote ourselves, our time, our talents and means for salvation of the human family.'

The purpose of the United Order as explained by one of the apostles was "each one for the whole, and God for all, an educational society for the industrious, frugal, and well behaved. It was for the strong to sustain the weak."

The settlements on the Little Colorado were advised by President Young to establish themselves under the United Order. Early in 1876, one of the settlers wrote: "It is all United Order here, and no beating around the bush, for it is the intention to go into it to the full meaning of the term." The United Order was based on the principle of cooperation. Essentially, each male member would donate all his possessions to the community and then devote his time and talents to promote the community's welfare. In a letter to Lot Smith, President Young emphasized the importance of commencing the United Order immediately in the Little Colorado settlements. He informed him that members sent to Arizona were carefully selected for the "express purpose of beginning and carrying on their labors of building and improving after the Order of Enoch." Articles of Association of the United Order were drawn up, and bylaws were formed by President Young and his counselors in 1874. Rules of conduct were detailed, and included for example, not swearing or speaking lightly of God or sacred matters, holding family prayer morning and evening, observing the Word of Wisdom, treating family members with kindness and affection, observing personal cleanliness, being chaste, refraining from all vulgar and obscene language. The rules further specified that members of the order should observe the Sabbath Day and keep it holy; and if they borrowed from a neighbor, they were to return promptly the borrowed article.

The Church historian of the Little Colorado settlements described the manner in which the system operated in the Allen Camp—later called St. Joseph, in honor of the Prophet Joseph Smith.

From the beginning, the Saints at Allen's Camp disciplined themselves strictly according to the rules of the Order. Every morning, at the sound of the triangle, the Saints assembled in the schoolhouse for prayer. On these occasions they would not only pray and sing but sometimes the brethren voiced brief remarks. The same practice was resorted to in the evening. They did not all eat at the same table (a common custom followed at the Sunset Camp presided over by Lot Smith), but nevertheless great union, peace, and love prevailed among the people, and none seemed to take advantage of his neighbor. Peace, harmony, and brotherly love characterized all the settlers at Allen's Camp from the very beginning. G. C. Wood of the Sunset settlement wrote in April 1876: "The brethren built a long shanty, with a long table in it, and all ate their meals together, worked together and got along finely."

When Elder Erastus Snow traveled from St. George to observe the progress of the Little Colorado settlements in September 1878, he was delighted with the remarkable organization operated in part under the United Order System at the settlement, then named Brigham City in honor of President Young headed by Jesse O. Ballenger. Part of it was enclosed in a fort 200 feet square, with rocky walls seven feet high— inside were 36 dwelling houses each 15 x 13 feet. On the north was the dining hall 80 x 20 feet, with two rows of tables to seat more than 150 persons. Adjoining was the kitchen, 25 x 20 feet, with an annexed bake house. Water was secured within the enclosure from two good wells. South of the fort were corrals and stockyards. The main industry was the farming of 274 acres. Milk was secured from 142 cows.

John Bushman, foreman of the community farm, describes how the United Order functioned. "The whole village," he wrote, "seemed more like one big family than a number of families. When anyone was sick or in trouble, all were ready to do anything they could to help." Some of the men were appointed to work on the farms, some to care for the stock and dairy. Others were to operate the sawmill and the tannery. Men and boys were assigned to do the gardening and distribute vegetables, others to care for the pigs and chickens. As the sheep herd increased, herders were charged to be the shepherds. Bushman added, "It was gratifying to note the willingness all showed to be obedient to the calls made upon them"

The four colonies established on the Little Colorado joined together to acquire a sawmill and start a tannery and dairy. Their most difficult task was to control the water from the turbulent river during flood seasons. Having dams swept away discouraged many, who then withdrew to Southern Arizona or back to Utah. Lot Smith wrote in poetic vein, "This is a strange country, belonging to a people whose lands the rivers have spoiled. Only for the United Order it is doubtful if any would have stayed along the river."

The son of President Brigham Young, John W. Young, visited the Little Colorado colonies in January 1878 and organized the colonists into a stake of Zion. Lot Smith was sustained president with Jacob Hamblin, who spent much time among the Indians, and Lorenzo Hatch as his counselors. A month after becoming stake president, Lot wrote the *Deseret News* concerning the workings of the United Order: "This mission," he penned, "has had a strange history so far, most who came having got weak in the back or knees and having gone home." He mentioned his preference for eating with his family, but as the entire community at Sunset ate their meals together, he had striven to show "that I was willing to enlarge as often as circumstances required, and the same feeling seems to prevail in these settlements." People passing along the Little Colorado stopped and boarded with the new settlers for a week or two at a time, "not withstanding our poor provisions and the queer style it was served up," concluded Lot.

Eating and working together, observed counselor Lorenzo Hatch, proved an order of Enoch condition of "no poor nor rich among us."

Over a year later, Apostle Wilford Woodruff came on official Church business to the Little Colorado settlements in May 1879. He was much impressed with the Saints living the United Order. He describes his visit with Lot Smith at Sunset:

I took my meals with him at the family table, the center table being forty-five feet in length and the side table being fifty feet, making three rows of persons. Each man has his place at the table with his family with him, the same as though he was with his family in his own house. Prayer is always offered at the table morning and evening before eating, and blessing is then asked. There seemed to be universal satisfaction among both male and female with the order of things. I conversed with several of the sisters. They preferred it to cooking at home. All fared alike, the president, the priest, and the people. If any were sick they were nourished. If any man was called on a mission, he had no anxiety about his family, knowing they would fare as well as the rest. If a man died his family would have the support as long as they lived with the people, and I must say that I felt in spirit that these settlements were living the United Order as near as any people could in mortality.

With President Lot Smith, Elder Woodruff rode muleback to Pleasant Valley in the pine and oak forest, thirty miles from Sunset. Here a thousand sheep grazed and were watered in large wooden troughs fed by clear, cold spring water. Because wildcats were numerous, the lambs were carefully watched day and night. The dairy operated by the United Order settlements was impressive, situated in one of the finest valleys of Arizona. On a horseback ride one evening, Elder Woodruff with Lot and others, saw fifteen deer, seventeen antelope, and five wild gobbler turkeys. A lumber mill operated at Millville had the capacity of sawing ten thousand feet of lumber daily. Groves of white oak, three feet in diameter, stood fifty feet in height. Lot Smith, as president of the Little Colorado Stake, had a large and thriving business under his supervision. He proved as capable, creative, and effective in this peaceful assignment as he had been as a soldier or wagon train raider. He was a versatile individual, capable of handling a variety of subjects, fields, and skills, turning with ease from one thing to another.

Lot Smith, both in public and private, was interesting and entertaining. His stake members could depend on him for sound doctrine and for wisdom in general matters. This wisdom he learned from the book of nature. He studied man, beast, and the wonders of God. He enjoyed life, although life on the Little Colorado brought him trials so sore that only angels could correctly reveal them, but his communion with God brought to him answers and solutions as though given to him directly by angelic messengers. While working at the grist mill, his right leg was crushed to pulp. For more than a year he suffered. Two of his sons died, one drowned in the river at flood time and the other was fatally scalded with lye water. What trials of faith came to the leader of the

Little Colorado Stake, but he never faltered or questioned the goodness of God.

Lot had his enemies, not among the Mormons, but among the Gentiles who came to trade with the Indians. One of them hired a desperado to kill him, but friends came to his rescue. To Lot, a treacherous man was an object of disgust and detestation.

CHAPTER 24

A Friend of the Indians

One of the reasons Lot Smith and his Mormon companions colonized the Little Colorado country was the potential conversion of the Hopi and Navajo Indians. The Book of Mormon, as the history of the forefathers of the Indians, was to be the principle tool of the Mormon missionary in the conversion of these people. Lot's first counselor, Jacob Hamblin, an apostle to the Lamanites, had mingled with the Hopis and Navajos largely as a peacemaker. With the assistance of such men as Thales Haskel, he had proven to the Indians that the Mormons were their friends; yet few were converted.

The colonists on the Little Colorado were instructed by President Young to treat the Indians kindly and with fairness but not to become familiar with them. The four settlements had erected forts for their protection and were always well armed, yet their relationship with the Indians was one of friendliness and helpfulness.

As a frontiersman, Lot Smith was unsurpassed. He was active and ambitious and performed noble work at Sunset in the interest of the Arizona Mission. His policy toward the Indians was that of the Prophet Brigham Young: "Feed them, not fight them." He received many letters filled with instruction from President Young which he read in meetings to the Saints and counseled them to carry out their leader's orders promptly. In one of the meetings with his fellow colonizers, President Lot Smith said: "All who feel like cursing an Indian and saying that the only good Indian is a dead one are released to go home."

Shortly after Lot and his fellow pioneers had settled at Sunset, they were visited by Chief Comah and other principal men of the Navajo tribe. Upon meeting Lot, the chief said through an interpreter: "We pleased you come and live here. Me know you heap good white man.

Me bringing my people to you—you show us how to raise wheat, corn, and cotton. Chief Tuba of the Hopi tribe, he cross great river to white man village with Jacob, our friend—he no speak with crooked tongue. White man show him big looms; white man make heap clothes from cotton; we want to plant cotton, so we can dress warm when snow come. You show us how to grow wheat, corn, and cotton?" This was reported by the Sunset chronicler, F. G. Nielson.

Lot was much pleased with the friendly, solicitous attitude of the Navajo chief and invited him to bring his people to Sunset where the Mormons would teach them how to plow and plant. Hundreds of Indians did come, and Lot and his brethren taught them how to farm. The Indians harvested twenty-five acres of grain the first season. Frihoff Nielson of Sunset gives the most information about the Indian farming. From his journal he noted: "Plowed in wheat for Indians. The Indians cleared the land. Indians worked on ditch today. Shocked wheat this morning, in afternoon binding. Many Indians here both Navajo and Moqui (what Hopis were called). They are gleaning wheat. Finished threshing today at noon. Have raised in all 2,515 bushels of wheat; 300 bushels of Moqui's wheat."

Lot visited the different tribes of Indians often. He inquired after their welfare and asked them if any of the Mormons were intruding on their lands or imposing on their rights.

Generally the Indians told him, "We glad you live here by us. Lot, you heap good white man. Mormons our friends."

Traveling fourteen miles from Sunset, Lot with other Mormon men came to the Hopi village of Walipi. Lot was impressed. The village, situated on the top of a fifty-foot-high mesa a hundred yards wide and four hundred yards long, was a grand sight to him. The village consisted of houses built one on top of the other the height of four stories. Three separate villages were grouped on the mesa with five thousand acres of land below the Mesa under cultivation. Corn, squash, and melons were growing well. These Indians packed their wood on the backs of donkeys for eight miles, then carried it up the ledge to their houses. Drinking water was also carried up the ledge.

After dark, a Navajo Indian came to the Hopi village and requested Lot to come to his village and "pray to the Great Spirit" for his daughter who was sick. Lot took John McLaws, who had been assigned to perform missionary work among the Indians. The next day the two men rode three miles southwest to the hogan of Tot-So-na-hasteen, head chief of the Navajos. Lot talked long to him, but the old Indian was not impressed. "Me no want Mormon religion!" While at the village Lot and John McLaws administered to the daughter of the Navajo Indian, and she was made well.

After the miracle about two hundred Navajo Indians gathered at the hogan of the chief. Men, women, and children came close to Lot. The children touched his trousers. The women felt his handmade coat. One lesser chief, Jualito, came up to Lot and eagerly inquired "You have book of our forefathers? Tell us about Great Spirit. How you come by book?"

Lot brought out a copy of the Book of Mormon from his saddlebags. "This book is a record of your forefathers. Your last chief—medicine man, you call him—came to a white man named Joseph Smith and gave him the record of your forefathers. Joseph Smith wrote this book into the language of white man." Lot and McLaws related to the Indians the message of the Book of Mormon.

Tears rolled down the cheeks of many Indians. One spoke out and said: "We know what you say is true. Our old men, who never lie, told us about our forefathers and what they say agree with what you say. Our forefathers did talk to Great Spirit. But they became wicked, fought one another. Good man—you call prophet—hid record in ground. We know not where, but you white men know."

The subchiefs rose up and embraced Lot and McLaws. "You good men—tell us of Great Spirit and forefathers. It makes our hearts glad," they said as they smote themselves on their breasts.

While Elder Woodruff was with the settlers on the Little Colorado he approached Lot Smith after he and McLaws had returned from the Navajo village where they had administered to the daughter of the Navajo man. He desired to visit a number of Mormon settlements in that country and to become acquainted with many Indian chiefs known to Lot, and requested Lot and others including Ammon M. Tequey, who had performed successful missionary work among the Indians to accompany him. Elder Woodruff readily observed that the persistency which had characterized his life was represented in the lives of the Saints they visited at Woodruff, a small town on the Little Colorado, named for him. An existence along the Little Colorado especially when it depended upon the performance of dams constructed on its quick sands, was both precarious and difficult. In late July Elder Woodruff and his associates went to Snowflake, where he joined President Jesse Smith in encouraging and strengthening the Saints in their most holy faith.

While at Snowflake in early August, the Apache Chief Pelone came to the Mormon town and invited the Apostle and other Mormon leaders to go hunting with him. On this occasion, though fond of hunting, Elder Woodruf was much more interested in preaching the gospel to the chief and other Indians than he was in pursuing the chase. At Elder Woodruff's request, Lot told Pelone and the other Indians with him about the Book of Mormon and the promises of the Lord respecting their forefathers.

On one visit with Pelone, Elder Woodruff related how he overheard Pelone give three young Mormon Elders the strongest rebuke he had ever heard from an Indian. The boys were smoking and asked Pelone to smoke with them. He looked them sternly in the face and said: "No, the Great Spirit has told me that if I would not smoke, nor drink whiskey, I should live a long time, but if I did I should live but a short time." Elder Woodruff said to the boys, "You should take that rebuke to heart and never again set such an example before an Indian."

Two days later Elder Woodruff, Lot, and Ammon talked with Pelone and an Indian named Pedro who was also an Apache chief, the two being principal chiefs of the tribe. Pelone had told Pedro all that he had been taught by the white men and appeared much interested in the message.

After visiting the Zunis, Lagumas, and the Isletas, the apostle told Lot that he considered these Indian tribes Nephites, a different race of people altogether from the Lamanites. These Indians were far above all the others, Navajos and Hopis included. The order of their houses and persons, their industry, their bearing and dignity in their talk with strangers, the expansion of their minds, and their capacity to receive the principles of the gospel fully equalled the ability, capacity, and the minds of the Anglo-Saxon race. Elder Tenney had baptized 155 Zunis. The Zuni village was much like the villages of the Hopis, built on elevated ground. Many of their dwellings were three stories high, the upper stories entered by ladders. Within the village of 3,000 souls there was "a heavy struggle between the Catholics and Mormon Zunis." The priests had lied about the Mormons. A few had apostatized, but the majority remained firm in the Mormon faith.

These Indians spoke Spanish. Lot was a capable interpreter and gave them good advice, encouraging them to ever show allegiance to the gospel of their Redeemer. Once he spoke to a gathering of Indian people for thirty minutes. When he stopped speaking to them, one arose and asked, "Why do you dismiss us? This is the first time we have heard of our forefathers and the gospel, and the things we have looked for from the traditions of our fathers. We want to hear more. We want you to talk all night; do not leave us so."

In November, cold weather settled in; and as the apostle, Lot Smith, and the others traveled through the mountains, the snow lay a foot deep. The wind pierced each man. They chopped down pine limbs, and improvised a shield to protect them from the winter blast. The men made their beds on the snow-covered earth. The night was extremely cold; and Lot, fearing that the horses might freeze, arose from his bed and brought them to the big fire which he kept ablaze almost all the night. It was December 1879.

On this cold journey, Elder Woodruff received a visit from President Brigham Young, who had died in 1877, in his dreams. He asked Brother Brigham if he would not address the Saints. The deceased President replied, "No, I am done talking in the flesh and that work is left to you, Elder Woodruff, and others to do." From the dream, Wilford quoted Brigham Young saying, "Tell the people to get the Spirit of the Lord and keep it with them."

By the spring of 1880, Lot had accompanied Elder Wilford Woodruff to Kanab. The apostle was returning to Church headquarters after spending nearly a year with the Saints in Arizona. In Kanab, Lot met a young man by the name of David King Udall, whom he requested to take the apostle to St. George with his best team of horses and carriage. Later, after Udall was called to settle with the Saints along the Little Colorado, Lot invited him to choose a span of mares from a band of fine horses as a token of appreciation for his service to Elder Woodruff. Lot told him, "I have done this because you have eyes that can see and a heart that can feel."

David Udall saw in Lot Smith a strong man physically, mentally, and spiritually, a warrior by nature, often misunderstood, but a true friend to the people over whom he presided. Lot proved to be a natural economist and homebuilder. Through his thrift and foresight, the United Order built up large flocks and herds, ranches, mills, and farms. Had the people possessed the dedication, strength and endurance of their leader, Lot Smith, and continued unitedly with the United Order, they would have become a great and wealthy people.

Existence along the Little Colorado, depending as it did on the dams which could only be constructed on its quicksands, was precarious and difficult. By 1885 the sandy land and the difficulty of irrigating it had driven the settlers away. Lot Smith and his family were the only ones left upon the ground at Sunset. Lydia's health was poor, even though she was only in her fifties. Lot arranged for her and two of his wives, Jane and Julian, to return to Farmington, Utah, keeping with him Laura, Ann, and Alice who had small children. Little did he and his childhood sweetheart, Lydia, know that their departure from each other would be the last time they would see one other in mortality.

About the time Sunset was abandoned, the Edmunds-Tucker Bill was passed by Congress. The year was 1886. It established polygamy as a continuous offense against the Constitution under the title of unlawful cohabitation or living with more than one wife. It abolished woman suffrage among the Mormons and dissolved the Church as a corporation. A large part of Church property was escheated, and an odious test oath, "Are you a Mormon or sympathetic with them," was imposed on all voters. Many of the Church leaders went into hiding, for the United States marshals were arresting every polygamist and the courts were imposing penitentiary sentences. Wilford Woodruff wrote Lot, informing him that President John Taylor had gone into voluntary exile. He advised Lot to flee with his family to Mexico. A decade before

1878, a Church mission had been opened in Juarez and a few years later the settlement of Mormon colonies from Utah were affirmed in the northern part of the Mexican republic.

Lot took his two wives and children and travelled to Juarez, Mexico, for there were no laws there prohibiting the practice of polygamy. In 1890 Wilford Woodruff, president of the Church, issued a proclamation known as the Manifesto prohibiting the practice of plural marriage among the Mormons. Learning of the issuance of the Manifesto, Lot Smith moved his family back into Arizona, knowing he would not be arrested and imprisoned for an offense now abolished.

CHAPTER 25

The Tragic End of Lot Smith

In September of 1878, Erastus Snow drove down from St. George in Utah to survey the Mormon holding in Moen Kopie. There were nine families living there. They had experienced a prosperous season in a farming way. On 17 September, Elder Snow with Andrew S. Gibbons and other Mormon brethren rode two miles west of Moen Kopie and located a townsite at Musha Springs. The Mormon settlers assured Chief Tuba, a Hopi Chief and a converted Mormon, that the place of settlement would be named in his honor. A few years later it was given the name of Tuba City

When Lot, his two wives and children arrived at the site of Sunset on the Little Colorado in June 1890, he drove to the house he once lived in. The premises were covered with weeds and drifted sand, but nearby the house and some running gears stood untouched and in good condition. Having decided to make his home in Moen Kopie, and having an extra team with him, he left his wives and younger children at the old house in Sunset and taking his two teenage sons with him drove the extra team pulling the running gears up to Millville where once the Saints had operated a sawmill. To his delight he found considerable slabs of lumber scattered about. He and his sons gathered up the limbs and loaded the sawed timber onto the running gears.

"Well, Pa, we got a full load of lumber," observed one of his teenagers.

"We sure have, son," replied Lot, patting him on the head, "You and James surely worked hard. Now we'll go back to Sunset, get your moms and travel on to Moen Kopie where the three of us will build the best house we've ever had to live in."

A turkey gobbled on the fringe of the forest a short distance from them. Seeing the turkey Burt whispered, "Pa, there's a turkey. I'm hungry. Shoot it and let's have a feast. What we don't eat we can take to our moms and the little children."

Moistening his trigger finger on his lips Lot took careful aim and pulled the trigger, and the big turkey gobbler toppled over. In a few minutes Burton and James had the turkey in their arms and laid at the feet of Pa Lot. Soon he had it cleaned, the feathers plucked, and each of them were roasting a choice cut over the campfire. Having a little flour with them Lot made some of his biscuits. It seemed to each one, man and boys, there had never been such a dinner or food so tasty. Lot and his sons hitched up the team. The horses had fed on the tall nutritious grass growing abundantly in Pleasant Valley and drank from a fresh stream of water flowing nearby. The boys filled their jugs full of the cold spring water. One of the lads commented, "We'll take our moms a fresh drink of water, and let the little ones sip some of this refreshing liquid from the spring."

Lot greeted his wives, Laura and Alice, with a warm embrace and hugged his children lovingly when they arrived at Sunset. "The boys and I got a load of lumber so tomorrow we'll drive to Moen Kopie," Lot told them. They invited him to see what they had found while he and the boys were at Millville. Back of the wagon they pointed to a hand plow, a pair of double trees, a copper kettle, and a shovel. "Where did you get these valuable items?" asked Lot. Smilingly Laura replied, "While you were gone we scoured the weeds and debris and found these useful things. How I missed the copper kettle when we drove to Mexico is beyond me."

"We'll surely use them in Moen Kopie," concurred Lot.

Two days later Lot and his family were eagerly greeted by Tuba, chief of the Hopi Indians. "Friend Lot, very glad to see you. You, squaws, and papooses going to live out here with us?"

After a warm embrace, Lot replied: "Yes, Chief Tuba, we'll make our home here the rest of our mortal lives."

"Mormon brethren gone to Musha Springs and built village. It two miles west of here. You go there maybe?" said Tuba.

"Yes, we'll move with our brethren, but we want you and your Hopi people to join us in farming and stock raising," returned Lot.

As Lot and his family with their two wagons and running gears loaded with lumber, pulled up to the fort at Musha Springs, they were met and welcomed by the Gibbons, the John Youngs, the Iversons, and Blythes. Following the welcome greeting the Smiths were shown a building lot on the south portion of the village and later Lot was taken a short distance from Musha Springs, where farming and grazing land were apportioned him. Assisted by his brethren, Lot built what was for those days a good-sized dwelling, with stone foundation and the walls and roof of lumber. It measured 30 by 60 feet, with a lean-to serving as kitchen and dining area. Alice and Laura, with their children, fit in congenially with the other sisters and the youth of the village. Lot took his sons and rode to several Hopi and Navajo villages to renew his friendly relationship with the Indians of the two tribes.

But Lot observed much to his dismay that relations between the Indians and the Mormon settlers were marked by tension and misunderstanding. A dam built by the colonists for the Indians broke and flooded some of the Indian farms. Enraged and furious over the loss of their crops, the Indians expected and insisted the Mormons to make good their loss. Mormon missionary zeal cooled considerably when the whites discovered the lack of interest and enthusiasm on the part of the Hopis and Navajos about performing hard labor in clearing the land, fencing, plowing, and planting. The Indians, mostly the younger men, were not in favor of the white man's expansion into their lands. One chief declared: "Water scarce—too many sheep, too many white people—we no want you to build more houses by our springs, but we want to live by you as friends."

With the encouragement of John W. Young, who had served as the first counselor to his father Brigham Young in the First Presidency of the Church before his father died in 1877, Lot Smith built a weaving industry at Musha Springs. The Hopis and Navajos had many sheep, wool was plentiful, and some of these Indians did weaving by hand. So a factory was erected and machinery installed, but the venture proved unsuccessful, much to the disappointment of Chief Tuba and his wife who had seen the huge looms and their effective operation in Utah's Dixie. Long before, in December 1870, Jacob Hamblin took the Tubas to the Mormon Cotton Factory in Washington, Utah. When Tuba beheld 360 spindles in action all at the same time, he had signed as he told Jacob he had no heart to spin with his fingers any more. He had expected Lot's machines to operate that well, and when they did not the old chief was frustrated.

Further contact with the Indians in the Moen Kopie area revealed to Lot a different type of Navajo than he had once known. Here he found Indians who respected neither the rights of the red men nor the whites. Many of them lived in the Navajo Mountains among the renegades who nurtured malice to the whites and had ravaged white settlements in southern Utah, killing some people, and driving off stock, then fleeing across the Colorado River into Arizona and hiding in the Navajo Mountains. These renegades being more powerful than the Paiute Indians who inhabited the Utah side of the river would compel the less powerful tribe to do their bidding. Frequently they also captured and made slaves of some of them.

In order to provide grazing for his herds of cattle, bands of horses and flocks of sheep, James M. Whitmore located and improved the Pipe Springs Ranch, which was fifty-five miles east from St. George and twenty miles west from Kanab. Whitmore employed a young man, Robert McIntire. On this certain occasion, snow was falling and the Navajos having crossed the river compelled the Pahutes under Chief Shevete, who were camped in the neighborhood, to assist in the killing of Whitmore and McIntire as they rode out in the falling snow to gather their stock. The Navajo renegades drove their sheep, horses, and cattle over the Colorado River, and they were never recovered. This is but one of many depredations on the whites in southern Utah. Some of the mares stolen by the Navajo renegades were valued from $100 to $250 each. Lot became deeply concerned about the welfare and safety of the Saints who had settled at Musha Springs; he didn't worry his wives and children about the precarious condition, but made definite plans at the most opportune time to move his wives and children to Utah.

While living at Musha Springs, Lot had more time to spend with his wives and children. He felt the need to teach and prepare his sons especially, for any eventuality. Almost daily Lot counseled with his sons. "I want you to be strong and courageous, care for your mothers and watch over your younger brothers and sisters. Be not afraid."

He taught them that whenever they faced situations where there seemed no way out, they must look up to the Lord and listen. He read with them Doctrine and Covenants 63:1 and taught them the words of the Lord and applied them to themselves, "Open your hearts and give ear from afar; and listen, you that call yourselves the people of the Lord, and hear the word of the Lord and his will concerning you." Then he commented, "We must learn to ponder, to pray and listen to the still small voice of the Holy Ghost."

Burt asked, "Where do you hear the words of the Lord, Pa?"

As Lot folded his young son in his arms, he said, "Son, we hear His word in reading the scriptures. I'd like you to pattern your life after the young man Nephi. Remember these words." He turned the pages in the Book of Mormon and read to his sons from 2 Nephi 4:15-16, "For my soul delighteth in the scriptures, and my heart pondereth them. . . . Behold, my soul delighteth in the things of the Lord; and my heart pondereth continually upon the things which I have seen and heard."

"Now sons, no matter what happens, and there will come unpleasant happenings, trust in the Lord, and keep the faith of your father. Please care for your mothers and younger brothers and sisters. I desire you boys to acquire good educations. We'll send you to the Eastern States to college but remember the words of Jacob, the brother of Nephi: "To be learned is good if ye hearken unto the counsel of God." (2 Nephi 9:28.)

Then with much feeling Lot told his sons, his wives, and all the children, "I love you for what you are, but I love you even more for what you are going to be.

"How I would enjoy seeing my wives and children in Farmington. We have engendered a love for one another in the plural wife relationship we'd never experienced without living in the combined family association."

"You'll see them next year, Pa, when we move north into Utah," spoke up James.

"That is my hope," said his father, "but sometimes hope is shattered."

Lot gathered his family about him in prayer daily. One evening after prayers as he rose from his knees, Lot said most solemnly to his family. "Of late, I have felt within me the future life. The sun's rays bathe us with its warmth, the earth gives us our sustenance, but from the heavens I have been illuminated with sounds of the future life. But please sustain yourselves with the faith that life is real and more lasting than earth life."

A short time after the failure of the knitting factory at Musha Springs, in the year 1891, a Gentile trader came into Lot's neighborhood to buy the wool clipped from the Navajos' sheep. He went by the name of Butch Swindle and became the friend of Father Neal Teel, the Catholic padre who tried to "Christianize" the Indians. Father Teel had observed the influence of the Mormons on Indian life and was jealous of that influence. Noting the tendencies of the younger Indian men to encroach upon the Mormon land, he used his influence to aggravate the rift. Both he and Swindle resolved to rid the Indian country of the Mormons. The padre said to the trader, "The Mormons must go or we will never control to our likes these Indians."

With a diabolic frown, Swindle said, "Leave it to me, Father. We'll get rid of Smith. He has too tarnation much power with the Indians. Leave it to me."

Trader Butch ingratiated himself with the Navajos, telling the young men, "You have as much right to the grazing lands outside your reservation as the d— whites. Your sheep are free to pasture along with the white men's cattle." He so excited the young bucks that they drove off a white non-Mormon rancher so that they could wash and shear their sheep there—with Trader Butch getting the wool.

The older Navajos strongly disapproved of the influence of the trader upon their young men but were unable to control their reckless tendencies.

C. L. Christensen, a Navajo interpreter and Indian missionary who lived at Moen Kopi at the same time as Lot, became Lot's intimate friend. Years afterward he wrote: "While I lived in Moen Kopi eight years, I saw them, the Navajo Indians, let their sheep into gardens and orchards, breaking fruit trees till they died; and all we could do was only to plead with them kindly, sometimes with good effect for a time, but soon this failed. They'd steal fruit, melons, grain in the shock, corn in the field, ride on our horses, stealing the bells from their necks, the hobbles from their legs, breaking the dams in our reservoirs, destroying our crops and causing the loss of our water and a hundred other things. Brother Lot Smith passed through all this and more also."

On a certain morning in June 1892, a haughty young Navajo told D. Claws, a non-Mormon, and other white men, five miles out of Musha Springs, Tuba, that "Maybe, pretty soon, Navajos kill and clear out some white men. We young Navajo braves talk about this for two days. You wait and see," he continued. Claws laughed at the Indian and made light of his threat, considering it to be a joke. But the Navajo stood tall in his moccasins and with threatening determination grimaced, "We kill one white man, anyhow." Swinging himself over the back of his mount he galloped off toward Moen Kopie. On Monday, June 20, 1892, Lot had the impulse to ride out to his pasture to see how his stock were. But throbbing in his soul were the words of a poet he had recently read to his family:

> Then stay at home, my heart and rest;
> The bird is safest in it's nest,
> Over all that flutter their wings and fly
> A hawk is hovering in the sky;
> To stay at home is best.

"Hawk," pensively mused Lot, "Why does it bother me?" He flung the thought away as he mounted his horse and rode out to his pasture. Arriving he saw the bars of his gate down. Navajo sheep were grazing with his cows. He tried to drive the sheep out of the pastures then put the bars up on his gate, but the sheep "bunched up" and he could not succeed. Angered, Lot rode back to the house and returned with a revolver in his belt. He dismounted and endeavored to drive the sheep from his pasture; but failing again, he drew out his revolver and fired several times into the flock, killing six sheep. In a moment, over the hill rode a half-dozen Navajos into Lot's field and fired into his herd, killing five cows. Other Indians appeared over the hill.

Lot started for his home on horseback to obtain help. As he rode past a large rock by the side of the dirt road, an Indian who had ridden up the hill ahead of Lot and waited in ambush for him to pass the rock, fired from behind it, striking Lot in the back, the ball going through his body at a slanting angle. Mortally wounded, the resolute Lot rode on toward home, the blood spurting in a stream from the open wound. Seeing a white man, who was none other than D. Claws, Lot beckoned to him; and the man raced to his side and helped hold him in the saddle as he rode rapidly to his house. How distraught was Claws when he saw the fulfillment of the haughty young Navajo's boastful threat "to kill one white man," and that he [Claws] had laughed it off as a joke, instead of warning the Mormons, especially Lot Smith. He could have saved his life.

Lot alighted from his horse, entered the house, unbuckled his belt, and staggered into the bedroom without uttering a word. He gathered his family. Grief-stricken, Lot's wives and children who were home gathered at his bedside. Lot, pale from the loss of blood and weak almost beyond movement, gasped, "This is the last of me." His dying words were, "God bless my wives and children."

The majority of the Indians were very sorry, as Lot had always been their good friend. Lot died as he lived, defending the right, penned Andrew Jensen, Assistant Historian of the Church.

Our history is studded with heroic names. These names compose a roster from which every nation may choose one and say: He is ours! But there was only one hero named Lot Smith. He was the symbol of heroic qualities. His heroism comprised the brilliant triumph of the soul over the flesh, over fear, over poverty, over suffering; he feared not calumny, nor illness, but loved his wives and children whom he trusted to God. Having no fear of death, Lot showed heroism to be the glorious concentration of courage.

Bibliography

Bancroft, Hubert Howe. *History of Utah*. San Francisco, 1890.

Brown, James S. *Giant of the Lord*. Salt Lake City: Bookcraft, 1960.

Cowley, Matthias. *Wilford Woodruff: Life and Labors*. Salt Lake City: Bookcraft, 1964.

Hunter, Milton R. *Brigham Young the Colonizer*. Salt Lake City: Deseret News Press, 1941.

Jenson, Andrew. *L.D.S Biographical Encyclopedia*. 3 vols. Salt Lake City: Andrew Jenson History Publishers.

McClintock, James H. *Mormon Settlement in Arizona*. Phoenix, 1921.

McGavin, E. Cecil. *The Mormon Pioneers*. Salt Lake City: Stevens and Wallis Inc., 1947.

McIntyre, Myron G., and Barton, Noel R. *Christopher Layton: Colonizer, Statesman, Leader*. Christopher Layton Family, 1966.

Nibley, Preston. *Brigham Young: The Man and his Work*. Independence, Mo.: Zion Printing and Publishing Co., 1936.

Rich, Russell R. *Ensign to the Nations*. Provo, Ut.: Brigham Young University Publications, 1972.

Roberts, B. H. *A Comprehensive History of the Church*. 6 vols. Provo, Ut.: Brigham Young University, 1965.

Schindler, Harold. *Orrin Porter Rockwell: Man of God—Son of Thunder*. Salt Lake City: University of Utah Press, 1966.

Smith, Pauline Udall. *Captain Jefferson Hunt of the Mormon Battalion*. Salt Lake City: Nicholas G. Morgan Sr. Foundation, 1958.

Tanner, George S. and Richards J. Morris. *Colonization on the Little Colorado: The Joseph City Region*. Flagstaff, Az: Northern Arizona University, 1977.

Wells, Junius F., ed. and pub. *The Contributor* (Representing the Young Men and Young Ladies Mutual Improvement Associations). Vols. 3-4. Deseret News Co., 1883.

This book is based on the life of Lot Smith and, as the above references suggest, this book has been carefully researched; however, as this book is a fictionalized account of Lot Smith's life, not every detail will be accurate.

2900

1st Ed
1st print